Internationally acclaimed author Suniti Namjoshi is an important figure in contemporary literature in English. A writer of fables, poetry, satirical fiction and children's fiction, she has published over 30 titles in India, Australia, Canada and Britain. Born in Mumbai in 1941, she first wrote and published in India, then moved to Canada, and then to a small seaside village in the south-west of England with writer, Gillian Hanscombe. In 2023, she was elected a Fellow of the Royal Society of Literature. Her books include *Feminist Fables*, *Goja*, *Suki*, *Aesop the Fox* and *Blue and Other Stories* from Spinifex.

Other books by Suniti Namjoshi

Feminist Fables (1993)
St Suniti and the Dragon (1993)
Building Babel (1996)
Goja (2000)
The Fabulous Feminist (2012)
Blue and Other Stories (2012)
Suki (2014)
Aesop the Fox (2018)

THE
GOOD-HEARTED
GARDENERS

Suniti Namjoshi

We respectfully acknowledge the wisdom of Aboriginal and
Torres Strait Islander peoples and their custodianship of the lands
and waterways. The Countries on which Spinifex offices are
situated are Djiru, Bunurong and Wurundjeri, Wadawurrung,
Gundungarra and Noongar.

First published by Spinifex Press, 2023

Spinifex Press Pty Ltd
PO Box 200, Little River, VIC 3211, Australia
PO Box 105, Mission Beach, QLD 4852, Australia

women@spinifexpress.com.au
www.spinifexpress.com.au

Edited by Susan Hawthorne, Pauline Hopkins and Renate Klein
Cover design by Deb Snibson
Typesetting by Helen Christie, Blue Wren Books
Typeset in Adobe Garamond
Printed in the USA

A catalogue record for this
book is available from the
National Library of Australia

ISBN: 9781922964007 (paperback)
ISBN: 9781922964014 (ebook)

For Alice

Learn of the green world what can be thy place
In scaled invention or true artistry,
Pull down thy vanity,
Paquin pull down!
The green casque has outdone your elegance.

Canto LXXXI, Ezra Pound

Contents

An Explanation

I don't know why I fell in love with Sybil. I thought perhaps she would improve my English. My English is good, but I grew up in India, and she's a native speaker, living in her native land. Or perhaps it was because I liked being in love. The euphoria permeated everything. When I asked why she had chosen me, she said, "Because you were there." Not the right answer. Then she said, "Well, for what did you want to be fallen in love with?"

We were neighbours. There was a small hole in the fence. And so I decided we were like Pyramus and Thisbe. In the beginning it was a literary love affair. She quite liked that. She dabbled in words and in love affairs. Like me?

But all that changed when the words mutated, ran rampant, and everyone – you'd better believe it – almost everyone spoke the same language. Only everyone had their own brand and their own voice, even if it was only a tiny whisper. The result was revolution.

All I had wanted was to be a good poet, master words. In short, be boss – like Humpty Dumpty, make words mean what I wanted them to mean. I wasn't expecting a change in the world order, or even wanting one. I got caught up like everyone else.

1

She's either very tall
or standing on a ladder

I've fallen in love with the woman next door. I intend to be in love in the same way that an astronomer is in love with the stars. There's ardour, there's fire. There's even the unattainability of courtly love. And there's also the cool, quiet, unimpeachable light of the scientist's gaze. I peer at my neighbour through a hole in the fence. I don't use a telescope. That would be cheating.

I walk into the back garden. I bend over to peer through the peep-hole and feel a leafy frond being swished around my head. She's looking down at me. She's either very tall or standing on a ladder.

There's no point in pretending I wasn't peering. She was peering too, worse than peering. She wasn't even discreet.

"Come and have tea?" she says. "I was just going to make some."

Wasn't that exactly what I was angling for? Still, it's disconcerting when the fish leaps and invites you to tea. I've fallen on my feet or else just fallen.

To make a good impression, I present myself as an unassuming, self-deprecating poet. She comes across as a tolerant woman.

We sit in the garden and drink tea.

"I'm Demo," I say.

"Short for?"

I don't want to tell her my real name. It's Damyanta meaning 'self control'. When I tell people that, they suppress a smile and shorten it to Dummy.

"Short for The Demolition Demon," I say assertively.

"I'm Sybil," she replies. I turn the name over and decide it's a good name.

"What do you do?" I ask.

"Garden, write the occasional poem. For a living I work on a dictionary project."

A dictionary project? I may have been mistaken. Could she be the enemy? Or an ally?

"I ought to warn you," I inform her. I know I'm showing off, but I want to make an impression. "I swing at rigid structures with a gigantic wrecking ball. I turn them into rubble. I liquefy language."

"I don't approve of wholesale destruction," she replies unperturbed.

"I dislike dictionaries …" I let my voice trail away. I can't very well say, "I had hoped to be lovers." I add lamely, "You are a preserver of words, whereas I want to make them malleable; so I suppose we can't be friends."

"It doesn't follow," she says mildly.

I shrug. "If we are enemies, we can't be friends. It follows all right."

"I thought you were in the business of crushing categories and pulverising nouns?"

Is she making fun of me? I decide to be nice, at least for the time it takes to drink a cup of tea. Then I can walk out.

Just as I am about to make my exit, she says quietly, "I haven't agreed to be your enemy. Do you dislike poems? And words as well?"

"Oh no." I relax, expand, explain myself, "I'm a poet too. Don't misunderstand. I'm not making a war on words. I like words, I want them to come up to me and eat from my hand, be pliant and biddable —"

I break off. She probably believes in hard definitions. She says, "Surely, precision matters?"

"Within the poem and in all its facets. But I want words to mean —" I stop short and start again more reasonably, "Would you show me your poems?"

"No," she retorts. "I don't trust you." Just like that, in so many words. Why is she being so rude to me?

"Why are you being so rude to me?" I demand.

"I'm not being rude, just circumspect," she replies. "You're not to be trusted. I overheard you reading aloud to your imaginary readers." So, she wasn't just peep-holing, she was eavesdropping as well. But calling my readers 'imaginary' has really annoyed me.

"My imaginary readers! He, she or even they might soon materialise – by the thousands!" I retort.

I get up. It's definitely time to leave. I've made a mistake. But then she says, "Don't leave in a huff. I thought you had decided to fall in love with me? Don't you like me anymore?"

"I don't like *me* anymore," I tell her. "I don't like who I've become in your eyes."

"Oh? Why don't I change you then?" she says sweetly.

Does she know how outrageous she's being? I'm sure she does.

Before I can reply, she carries on, "Don't be cross. Without our frippery, we're just barking egos, rolling over to have our tummies tickled, and the next minute snapping and snarling. Why don't you allow me to deck you with words, adorn you with adjectives? I could write you a poem?"

"I was going to write you a poem!" I've blurted that out before I could stop myself.

"Were you?" she says with a faint lift of her eyebrows.

When the hunter becomes the prey? I had never intended to hunt. Had I?

"Don't you like me as I am?" I've blurted that out too. And I know what she's going to say.

She says it. "I thought you weren't rigid? Were capable of change?" She's lying back in her chair looking up at me. I'm on my feet, ready to leave, not ready to leave. Suddenly she rises and puts her hands on my shoulders.

Shall I cast you a spell?
Make you a mirror?
Teach it to tell
      delicious untruths
on which you can dwell?

"I can play that game," I reply.

To slip into the water
and turn into ourselves,
won't that do as well?

We pull ourselves together. "Why can't *you* change yourself?" I ask her. "Tell me I'm wonderful and believe it?"

"I adore you," she says, drawing closer, so that I breathe her in, can almost feel the texture of her skin. I realise we've been watching each other for days.

She pushes me back. "But that bee in your bonnet! That has to go."

"In my bonnet? A bee?" I ask worriedly.

"Yes," she replies, still smiling, "The Liquefaction of Language."

"My mission – a cliché, a peccadillo, at best an eccentricity?" I look at her plaintively.

"Dispense with words?" she murmurs.

At dawn, I scramble over the fence and into my own garden. I could have walked around, let myself in with the latchkey. But I feel like a troubadour. I could write an aubade. I could be John Donne and scold the sun. Though it would be better to be Sappho. I could be myself. The next day Sybil and I cut a hole in the fence, hidden by shrubs on either side.

2

Like a set of false teeth

Jack Stickler sticks to the rules. Sybil explains he's a friend and a member of her Gardeners' Club. He's complaining about people who want to call themselves 'they', when 'it' will do. I point out they might be engaged in a process. True metamorphs?

"Besides," I say to him, "what would you do with a plurality of 'its'?"

"That doesn't matter."

"What does matter?"

"Linguistic propriety," he answers instantly. I dislike him on the spot. What is he doing in Sibyl's garden? Why has she bothered to introduce him? She tells me later she thought we might have something in common. Was she teasing me?

In my opinion Sibyl's garden has too many visitors. I don't mean the blackbirds and the robins, the blue tits and finches. I can ignore them. Later that day I peer through the peep-hole. Is it too early to see if she's about? I stare at the tightly curled peonies. The irises are in bloom. I know it's ridiculous, we've only just met, but I long to see her; and suddenly she's there talking to me from the other side. I press my lips against the fence.

"What are you doing?" she asks.

"Trying to kiss you," I mumble.

"Silly," she says, but her voice is indulgent. "Come and help me."

"With what?"

"With making a hole in the fence."

I get a shovel and a saw, and as soon the gap is large enough, I crawl through. "Like a serpent," she says looking down at me.

"In paradise," I say looking up at her, hoping that's the right thing to say. But I don't really like being called a snake. Is calling people names a metamorphic act?

"Help me with the garden," she commands.

I dig up dandelions. Sybil beside me is weeding too. She allows me to kiss her. We topple over and lie there like a pair of myna birds – wrong country, never mind – unable to extricate ourselves. Is Sybil a word or a person, and how do I want to shape her? I don't. All I want is to be with her and let time lap against us and shape us as it likes.

We're interrupted by a woman bustling through the garden. She goes straight into the greenhouse and emerges with a tray of seedlings. She's quite unembarrassed by the sight of us. Sybil too appears unembarrassed. I decide to be unembarrassed as well. "This is Camilla," Sybil tells me. I stare at Camilla. Her skin tone is the same as mine. A fellow Indian?

"You mean, Kamala!" I say before I can stop myself.

"No, Kamilla," she informs me, "with a K. And you are?"

"Demo," Sybil tell her, "The Demolition Demon."

"And what do you do, Demo?" Kamilla asks.

By this time we've got to our feet. "Oh, Demo's a radical," Sybil answers carelessly. "She digs up dandelions, makes war on buttercups, roots out bindweed in an effort to create a better world, don't you, my love?"

I can only mutter, "So to speak, of course."

"Ah, we are speaking analogically, I see," Kamilla replies, just to make it clear she knows what's going on.

"The Garden Scene, *Richard II*," Sybil interjects helpfully. For some reason she seems to think it's all a joke.

"I, myself, am a conservationist," Kamilla informs me. "I don't eradicate. I nurture what's there. You may call me Kams for short."

I don't want to call her anything. "What?" I say, pretending to be astonished and glancing at her tray. "No pricking of seedlings? No judicious murders? No ridding yourself of unwanted extras?"

"Well, of course," she says. "The original strain must be kept strong." She's feeling nettled. "The difference is you uproot. I conserve."

"I eradicate your enemies," I say sweetly, "unloved weeds that would overrun the garden."

"There are many wildflowers that are acceptable. Primroses, for example, and native bluebells," she tells me primly.

Sybil intervenes. "Kams is very knowledgeable. Left to my own devices I'd let everything grow. And then where would we be? In a jungle!"

She laughs and I'm charmed by the curve of her lips. Distracted, I contemplate the mass of exuberant greenery, not caring in the least about well-kept gardens.

Kams is appeased. "Yes," she says smugly. "I help Sybil cultivate her garden." She looks at me as though to say she has prior rights.

Suddenly I'm annoyed. Why is she cultivating Sibyl's garden? My darling 'is all states, all princes, I,' or something of the sort. Eventually Kamilla leaves with her tray of seedlings. I glare after her. But then I look at Sibyl and forget about Kams.

We go into the greenhouse. I can hear the grass murmur. Is it the grass or us? Or a memory of Sappho's poem?

"Do you love me?" asks Sybil.

"Yes!" I reply happily. What could be clearer?

"Warts and all?" she continues.

I hesitate. I don't like warts. "Yes," I reply.

She nibbles my ear. "Would you love me still," she wants to know, "if I told you just 'between you and I' that I neither conjugate nor decline?"

"I would try," I say awkwardly. It's not the right answer. She knows I hate it when people misuse language. Metamorphosis is not the same as mutilation. What's she getting at?

"Who are you in love with," she teases, "me or your image of me?"

"Without words how could I know you? Perhaps you would only be a heady sensation."

"Heady, but imperfect?"

"Love is not love when it imperfection finds," I mutter. But then she kisses me. I stop thinking altogether, until she whispers in my ear, "I told you you had something in common with Jack."

I ignore that, but the next morning we have an argument. I'm enjoying my breakfast – pancakes with maple syrup and crisp bacon – when she says, "You're my lovable limpet, my sweet snufflebag." She's being fond, even flirtatious. Does she want to fall into bed all over again? I'm willing. But I don't like being called a limpet or a snufflebag.

I ask conversationally, "How can you like words in general? The currency is teeming with counterfeit coins."

She seizes on that. "'Teeming' you said. So alive, not dead. Capable of regeneration."

"And of spawning mangled monsters," I snort at her.

I can see I've angered her. Her eyes flash. "An example," she snaps.

"Workaholic!" I retort.

"What's wrong with hybrids? You're a —," she stops short.

I'm furious. "Are you calling me a hybrid?" I demand. "I can trace my ancestry for at least seven generations – on both sides!" I shouldn't have said that. Now she'll think I'm a snob.

"That's not what I was about to say!"

"What then?"

"That you're talking like a prig, not a poet!"

"Anything else?"

"Yes. And like a prude and a pedant."

I'm so angry, I don't know what to say. She carries on more calmly, "Words need to be valued, their mutations noted. There's a word hoard inside your head. You've been meta-morphosing all your life."

"From what to what?" I interrupt furiously.

"From Indian into something English," she says. "Soon you'll be one of us."

Worse and worse. "And you think that is the summit of my ambition?" I say nastily.

"It's not an ambition," she replies. "It's a process. Don't be so cross. It's not a requirement."

"A requirement for what?"

"A requirement for being held in my arms and for writing poems."

But it is a requirement. Could we love each other without language?

"I'm not an embodiment of Englishness, you know," she says gently. "I'm changing too."

"You haven't even been to India!" I challenge her.

"Yes I have," she retorts. "And I can make curry with the best of them."

"So can the whole nation!" I retort.

She nods. "That's my point."

"There's an imbalance of power!"

"True," she says. "You outnumber us by hundreds of millions."

I don't know what to say to that. We eat in silence. After a while she says, "Tell me some other words you particularly dislike. 'Humongous?' 'Ginormous'?"

"'Like'," I spit out at her, "that mad monosyllable, which, like a set of false teeth, goes clacking about!"

She's taken aback. "What do you mean?" she asks.

"Like! Like! Like!" I'm on my feet now, and sound angry. Have I lost her? She'll decide I'm an ogre and never speak to me again. Perhaps I could recant? About what? No, I can't do that. Besides, she's been rude to me. I could break with her. But I don't want to lose her. I could keep my mouth shut? Say I've taken a vow of silence?

I'm amazed to find she's laughing.

"Do sit down," she says. "That's such a good rendition of a crazed chicken. You're right. That's one of the words I'm concerned about – the poor, little thing. Such a hard worker, and now done to death."

"Let it die! Off with its head!" I say brutally in keeping with my Destroyer avatar. I've just morphed the Queen of Hearts into Lord Shiva – is that allowed? She doesn't notice.

She shakes her head. "Can't do without it. Why did you say that?"

"What? 'Off with its head'? To see what it sounded like."

"You see?"

"What?"

"'Like'. You just used it."

I call a truce. "Perhaps you're right," I murmur. "Perhaps the young people are searching for an elusive metaphor, but then realise that the thing itself is more like itself than any comparison."

It's a peace offering. "Let's —?" I suggest.

"Later," she replies. Suddenly she's serious. "Words are so used and abused. They need to be tended."

"You think of words as though they were living things," I accuse her.

"You think of words as though they were plastic chips!" she shoots back.

"Analogies will get you nowhere," I growl.

"Analogies will get me everywhere. I have a friend, Ludo. He specialises in similes and metaphors. He picks them out and gobbles them up."

This time the twinge of jealousy is so sharp that words desert me. All I can say is, "Huh!"

"At a loss for words?" She's mocking me again.

I get up. "I'd best be going," I say stiffly.

But she pulls me down, and I give in. I'm not disinterested, I'm not consistent. I'm besotted.

3

Nobody has a private ocean

I hang about near the peep-hole, pretending to water flowers. I dig up a weed. No sign of Sybil. Kams enters. Sybil's garden is like a stage set – everyone wanders through! "Hey Demo," she calls. I pretend I'm not there.

"Hey Demo," she repeats. "Stop skulking. Sybil's gone away for a day or two with Lord Ludo. She asked me to keep an eye on things. I need a trowel. Can I borrow yours?" I throw a trowel over the fence. I hope it hits her. That was unworthy. I don't hope that. But Lord Ludo? I'm furious.

Sybil introduced him the other day. He was affable, tried to put me at ease, asked how long I was staying in the country. How dare he try to put me at ease! I want to ask Sybil if he's her lover. And also if Jack Stickler is her lover? And Kams? But something about Sybil discourages such questions. And I'm afraid of the answer. She might say, "Yes" or "Not at the moment."

I can't think straight. I go out and run into Nandu. Like me, he's loosely attached to one of the colleges. I doubt very much that he can help. He's a medievalist and what I need is an alchemist, someone who can provide an anti-love philtre.

We go into a pub, order our pints, and I tell him my woes while gazing moodily at the river.

"You could fall in love with someone else?" he offers.

"No!"

"You could stop being jealous and share her with Ludo or Kams or whoever?"

"Absolutely not!"

"Become a celibate? Devote yourself to good works or to your mission. What was it? The Liquidation of Language? Liquidate her. Delete the thought, the word, the noun."

"What? Abolish her?"

"No, she'd disappear for you, but she'd be there, alive and well, for everyone else."

"That's exactly what I don't want! I want her for myself! I need her," I protest. "Besides, my mission isn't liquidation, it's The Liquefaction of Language."

He's as useless as the ducks sitting on the riverbank.

He shrugs. "Language changes anyway. You don't need to help it along."

"I want control and I want the words to embody change."

"And how are you proposing to do that? By the continuous use of the continuous present as we Indians are constantly being accused of doing? You are not controlling the internet, or the mass media, or the curriculum; you are not even having millions of shekels. You're puny. You can rage. You can rant, but so can everyone else."

He's getting off on his own words. "Sorry. In time you'll feel better."

He pats me on the shoulder and goes back to his work. I walk along the riverbank, and consider throwing myself into the water. It looks uninviting. And anyway I am not that sort of poet. A part of me wonders whether it's my heart that's broken or my ego that's crushed.

That evening I get a text from Sybil. "Back soon. Gone with Ludo."

Without stopping to think, I zap right back. "I thought I was your lover?"

To which she says, "So what?"

"So you shouldn't go away with Ludo."

"Why?"

I don't know what to say to that. And then I ask a question I know it's dangerous to ask. "Is he your lover?"

To which she replies, "Yes. So's Jack Stickler. So is Camilla. And for all you know, I'm lying. And anyway, I don't belong to anyone."

No, she belongs to everyone! I don't text that. I have a drink, and then another and another. Eventually I fall asleep and wake up with a headache. I tell myself that it would be a sign of weakness to look at my phone. I look anyway. Nothing from Sybil.

I try to work. I write a poem, and against my better judgement I send it to her.

Sometimes you just leave like a mermaid
disappearing underwater or like an inter-
stellar traveller walking through a wormhole,
or like the sun dipping down, the stars winking out,
a dream breaking up,
                or like anything
and everything in this ephemeral world,
           and it hurts.

I get a reply, just two words: "I'm changeable."

And so she is. Then there's a second message. "Don't be so difficult. I particularly liked the interstellar traveller. Can't we be friends? I'm back tomorrow."

Friends! I calm down. She's right. I am confined by categories. Have to be civilised. I text back: "A good poem requires conventions."

To which she replies, "Also a bending of conventions."

I don't want to play. She may be within her rights, but humankind cannot bear too much freedom. I can't anyway. I tell her that and ask to be left alone. After that silence, a head full of poetic clichés and a hangover.

I go for a long walk, eat something, come back, tidy up the house and decide to go away for a few days. To London. I could go around the museums one by one, find an answer, at least not mind if there are no answers. I fall asleep eventually.

I dream about Sybil rising from the foam like Aphrodite or Lakshmi, surrounded by little fishes.

"Who are you?" I demand.

"The Queen of Conundrums. It's me, silly!" Teasing as usual.

"And who am I?"

"Just a poor fish, a very proper noun?"

"And the sea? Who controls it?"

"No one controls it. It's a free-for-all."

"Then why summon me? Why show yourself?"

"I didn't. You made me up."

"Don't you exist?"

"Of course I exist. I'm right in there, swimming beside you. Darling Demo, you miss what's obvious."

"Don't call me 'darling'. You've made it clear I'm of no consequence."

"Of course you are. Your problem is you want to be more consequential than anyone else."

"This sea we're swimming in? Is it life or literature?"

"Both. Someone makes words. Someone else understands them. The combined fish spawn is all around us."

Suddenly, I feel hopeful. "Is this a private ocean?"

She shakes her head. "Nobody has a private ocean."

I'm despondent again. "Then it's all over?"

"Why? Have you stopped loving me?"

"I can't own you, or control you. You're up for grabs."

"Just a poor fish then. Like you."

"Is this a different analogy? We're no longer in the garden?"

"We've taken to the water."

"And we're inconsequential lovers?"

"That's up to you."

"Sybil?"

"Yes?"

"Don't you love me at all?"

"I do. I adore you on Tuesday, but not on Thursdays."

"Sometimes I hate you."

"This is your dream. The words are all yours."

"In a communal ocean?"

The next morning I catch an early train. I don't know how the dream ended. She probably had the last word.

I check into a B&B, and walk to the nearest tube station. In the train I look around at my fellow passengers – the usual lot, some neat and clean, others not. I fit in easily, but so would anyone. Could any of them be my imaginary readers? How much of their experience do I want to share? Still, listening to someone going on about themselves isn't the same thing as reading a book. I get off at Euston and walk towards The British Library. There's that statue of Newton bent over his work. I go in and stare at the massive column of books. What will they do when more books have been published than their coffers can hold? Will they store them underground? They do that already. And after that? Do old books have to disappear to make room for the new? Language as well?

A friend once told me about a woman who died in the Andaman Islands and how, with her, her language died. I wrote a poem about her which she'll never read.

BOA SENIOR

On January 26, 2010, a woman named Boa Senior died in the Andaman Islands of India at the age of about 85. With her died a language called Bo and a world view and the wisdom of nearly 70,000 years. After the death of her parents, some 30 to 40 years earlier, Boa had become the lone speaker of the tribal language and she reportedly kept it alive by speaking to the sparrows.

T. Vijay Kumar

My father died, and one third of the words
                              went with him.
My mother took the next third.
                              I was left alone
with my diminished word hoard.
                              They looked like coins,
like a golden treasure.
                              Against whom should I
guard such unwanted stuff?
                              I spoke to the sparrows,
who told me nicely they didn't eat gold.
                              At least they understood me.
When it was my turn to go,
                              they scattered the words.

They've scattered English words all over the continents. Are words seeds? Coins? Fishes? Do coins beget coins? Money does.

I sit in the courtyard drinking cappuccino. I know it's not the way to imbibe learning. How does one learn anything? David Attenborough says that what distinguishes us as a species is our exceptional ability to create culture, that is, to tell each other what we've learnt. Does he mean we're good at talking? And what's the difference between being civilised and being cultured? I thought civilisation had to do with shoving and pushing to make ourselves comfortable. Hence global warming – we've made ourselves a little too comfortable. Culture is more a state of mind and like poetry makes nothing happen. Doesn't it? Doesn't it make the heart break? No, the heart breaks first, then the poems come. Always an effect, never the cause?

Is talking to people an intimate act? Every book should carry a warning: "Caveat lector. Your brain is about to be impinged upon."

I wish I could stop thinking about Sybil. How can I ask for constancy when we live in change? It isn't sensible.

4

One of the things I like about the English

On impulse I walk into the Ritblat Gallery, pick up a speaker and listen to Virginia Woolf. Her voice is icy, composed of sharp edges. I don't think people come back to haunt us. They were always there, swimming about in memory. Then memory disintegrates like an iceberg calving: people die, discs degrade, and entire civilisations are put to the sword. That's in the long term, but in my life span I'm floating in memory and Sybil Past, Present and Future are simultaneous. Is it for the sake of Sybil Past that I'm enamoured of Sybil Present? And is it for the sake of Sybil Present that I would willingly make extravagant promises to Sybil Future?

While I'm staring gloomily at a Pali manuscript I can't read, I hear my phone ping. The message says, "Come back. If you do, I'll pay you with my word hoard."

I'm not sure what to make of it. That doesn't stop me from answering: "Your word hoard is common currency. When Boa Senior died, her word hoard vanished."

"Who was she?"

I send her the poem. There's a reply. "She shared it with the sparrows."

"They weren't listening."

"You're not listening either."

Then without intending to, I write, "Why don't you come to London?"

And she agrees. She says, "All right" and asks where I am. By the time I get back to the B&B, she has arranged for a larger room and a double bed. We go out eventually, get something to eat, and return to consider what we might do tomorrow, how pass our long love's day. Is poetry sometimes both cause and effect?

In the morning, as soon as I'm awake, Sybil says to me, "I know the secret of the universe. It's composed of bubble clusters; the bubble clusters all impinge on one another and become a part of larger clusters."

"What happens if the bubbles break?"

"They just vanish leaving a residue in other bubbles."

"Are they permeable?"

"Semi-permeable," she replies.

"I'm not sure I want to live in a soap suds universe." Or a bubble wrap one, I think privately.

"Don't you?"

Suddenly I don't care which universe I live in. "Because I'm in love with you," I tell her, "I'm in love with everything, the whole universe."

She demurs, "That's too heavy a burden for one person to carry."

"All right, the whole world. Well, a part of it. This island."

She shakes her head. "I'm not a country, or a culture or a language. I'm a person."

At breakfast I ask Sybil, "Are your bubbles a description of atoms and molecules or are they words?"

She looks at me as though I don't know anything. "The universe isn't composed of words," she informs me. "Words are a net we throw at the universe to discern its shape."

"And if the words alter?"

"Then we think we have a different universe."

She may be right. I must think about it. My darling is clever. And gorgeous. It's impossible to describe how gorgeous she is, or how the fried eggs glow or how the milk has lustre. It's a painter's breakfast.

We take ourselves off to Kew by boat.

Blue skies today, not grey. The light falls on Sybil's hair so that some of the strands shine like metal. That's one of the things I like about the pink English and Caucasians in general: their hair can be different colours, and so can their eyes. Sybil's eyes change according to the clothes she wears. In a poem I would have to tell her they change with the weather.

At Kew we sit on a bench watching a coot scurrying back and forth, back and forth across the water with twigs for her nest, possibly his nest. I remind Sybil she had promised me a few words from her word hoard. She says I haven't earned them.

"Can't I have some anyway?"

She rummages in her handbag, retrieves a piece of plastic and puts it in my hand. Is she making fun of me? I look at her inquiringly.

"It's a building block," she explains.

"All right, words are building blocks. I accept that. But one word doesn't a palace make."

"Could do, might do if it was watered properly and had the right soil," she retorts.

Mixed metaphors. Deliberate obfuscation. She continues to rummage.

While I wait, I tell her about a book I've been reading about artificial intelligence. Relying on the words of a linguist called Firth, the programmers decided that it would help machines to use ordinary English, if the machines knew which words often occurred together. "You shall know a word by the company it keeps," I quote darkly. I'm about to ask her to give me related words, when I remember that I don't know what she has given me already.

"Which word have you—" I begin. "No, wait. Don't tell me. Let me decide. I pronounce this a brick. Please give me a few more bricks."

I've decided to play it safe. I was afraid she would say she had given me the word for me, my 'self', my innermost being. I do not want to be defined by a piece of plastic. Have I a rigid self after all, one whose hackles rise at the slightest threat?

She extracts a few more plastic bricks and gives them to me. Why does she carry them in her bag? I don't question her. She'd probably say she was carrying them for me. I play with them and say. "Now you must imagine a stately dome and the walls of a palace rising from the ground – a bit like Versailles." This is hard. I don't know anything about architecture. How am I supposed to conjure a palace?

"Which is it going to be?" she wants to know. "Stately dome or Versailles?"

"Versailles," I reply hurriedly.

"And the gardens?" she demands.

"These?" I offer, looking around helplessly.

"I've made a mishmash, haven't I?" I admit ruefully. "Versailles set in Kew with a dome here and there." She laughs. "Anyway," I go on, "I've understood a thing or two about words."

"What?"

"They're dependent on what was already there."

"Not so. What's there is dependent on a word for it."

"That palace I built – words are made out of other words as well as existing objects. Things can be named, therefore they exist? Which came first, the chicken or the —"

She stops me with a kiss and we leave the coot to get on with her nest.

We're barely aware of which way we're walking. Wherever we look there's something pleasant – a glade, a pond, a venerable tree. I realise I'm happy. This moment I am happy and I do not know if I will ever be so happy again. I glance at Sybil. I hope she feels what I feel; not so much for my sake, as for hers. We walk on the grass, sit down, lean against a tree trunk and stare at the geese.

"Do you think it's allowed?" Sybil wonders.

"What?"

"Walking on grass. Leaning against tree trunks. Staring at geese. Being happy."

"We're allowed to be happy," I tell her.

"For how long?"

"For today," I reply.

A pair of blackbirds, who are busy with their own affairs, pause to look at us. "We're carefree," I inform them, "even more carefree than you are."

I stretch out and look up at her and at the sky. "Tell me a story," she says.

"About what?"

"About me."

"All right, I'll tell you a story about your namesake."

One day a foolhardy woman asked the Sybil for a plain answer to a plain question.

'Ask away,' said the Sybil wearily.

'When will I die?'

'On the 23rd of April 2022,' the Sybil told her. 'Now go away. As I myself am probably immortal, I find myself envying you.'

The woman went away. She knew she'd been lucky. The Sybil's answers were always problematic, that was well known. But here she'd been given a straightforward answer. No guesswork, no riddles, no double meanings. Just a plain hard fact. She ought to make the best use of it.

The foolhardy woman worked out she had exactly 7355 days of life left. She was appalled. That wasn't very much. She could count up to 7000. She decided to be careful. When friends came to visit, she would set a stop watch going. When five minutes were up, she would get up abruptly, say that she had just given them five minutes of her life and that she couldn't afford more. Usually the friends would leave without demur.

She pared down her sleep to just two hours a night. This made her feel crazy, but she didn't care. She took to changing her clothes just once a week and later not at all because that saved even more time. She stopped brushing her teeth. It was true her teeth would decay, but she had calculated that they would outlast her.

She thought about taking up skydiving or hang gliding or bungee jumping. After all, till the 23rd of April 2022 she was virtually immortal, but then remembered what had happened to the Sybil. She might not die; but that didn't mean she wouldn't get injured or incapacitated. She decided to try gambling instead. She had given up her job – why waste time? – and had worked out that if she lived frugally, her savings would take her to the last day of her life. But clearly, if she had more money, she could live more luxuriously. She went to a bookie and said to him, 'I'll make a bet with you that I'll die on the 23rd of April 2022. What odds will you give me?' The bookie turned her down. And this was just as well, because even if she had won, she would have found it impossible to collect.

She consoled herself by working out how much time she'd saved. 'I used to sleep for eight hours every night, but by sleeping for only two, for every four days I gain a whole day. And then there are the bits and pieces I've saved by bathing only once a month, and eating baked beans day in and day out (cooking time saved) and by never listening to music or watching movies or bothering with a job or looking at flowers or tending the garden. By now I must have saved a huge heap of time. I'll go ask the Sybil if it has made any difference to the day of my death.'

The Sybil glared. 'You again?'

'Got another question,' the woman said boldly. 'I've been ever so careful and I've saved a huge lot of time. I figure I've gained five years at least. So now, please tell me again, when will I die?'

'You'll die on the 22nd of February 2017,' the Sybil replied.

'But that's five years earlier!' the woman exclaimed. 'You said I would die on the 23rd of April 2022!' She stamped her foot. 'You can't change things just like that.' She was outraged by the unfairness of it all.

'I didn't change anything,' the Sybil snapped. 'You did.'

The woman's way of life had reduced her to skin and bones. She fell at the Sybil's feet. 'What went wrong?' she cried.

The Sybil shrugged. 'Nothing. It's just the same old story – knowledge without wisdom,' she replied coldly. But as she looked at the creature sobbing at her feet, she felt a twinge of fellow feeling – something she hadn't felt for hundreds of years. 'Your mistake was similar to mine when I asked

for eternal life without eternal youth. Now you must live
with it.'

'What must I live with?' wailed the woman. 'I know I
must die, but I can't be sure when.'

'Exactly,' said the Sybil, quite gently for her. 'That's how
it is.'

Sybil is outraged. "Are you calling me a bad-tempered old woman?"

"Not at all," I reply, "I'm calling you a semi-immortal who always gives problematic answers."

"There's no such thing as a 'semi-immortal' and all answers are problematic."

"There you are then," I say amicably.

We're about to fall into each other's arms again, but I hold back in case anyone's looking. She doesn't seem to worry about what she does. Perhaps it's because she's on home territory and feels confident that it will be all right. I'm more circumspect. We stand up and brush our clothes and get some lunch. We wander into a greenhouse. Sybil glances at me and informs me she likes exotics. I tell her I like natives. I suppose I could have said I like exotics too, but in which language? She has corrected my English twice this afternoon. When I said, 'ad*mir*able', she said, '*ad*mirable', and when I said, '*for*midable', she said 'for*mid*able', so I said she was both. Is it all a matter of contradiction and compromise? Do I want to change language and preserve it? Even in a poem I only have limited control. The imaginary readers, who haven't materialised yet, get a vote. I frown at Sybil, who rewards me with a smile. Impossible not to like her for that.

We catch the train back, eat something and fall into bed. The next morning we're thrown out of paradise.

5

The King's head

Sybil's in the shower. I'm half asleep. A phone pings. I reach across and pick it up. It's Sybil's phone with a message from Lord Ludo sprawled across it: "What have you discovered? Is she a spy?"

When Sybil emerges I hand her the phone. Perhaps she'll explain, perhaps not.

She says, "I have to go back right away."

What can I say? Has Sybil been toying with me? And what does 'toying' mean? It's not as though we had agreed to a lifelong commitment.

Sybil hesitates, then makes up her mind and sits down beside me. "It's not what you think. I have a proposition for you."

"A business proposition?" What's she on about?

"No, nothing like that. I belong to a secret organisation, an extension of MI5, though we might be moved to MI6. They're not sure what to do with us. Anyway, would you like to be a member of my cell?"

"Your cell! Are you a spy?" I demand.

"No, but we thought you might be one."

"Why would I want to be a spy? Who or what do you want me to join?"

"My gardening group," she says. "We are The Society for Well-Meaning Efforts for the Betterment of Language and the Salvation of the Planet. As a disguise we call ourselves The Good-Hearted Gardeners."

While I'm taking that in, she continues, "The others will have to approve of you. There's a meeting tomorrow. We're recruiting. Will you come?"

Join Ludo and the rest of them? Work for MI5? It's ridiculous.

"I suppose there would have been more kudos in it for you if I had been a spy you managed to turn?" I say bitterly.

She laughs. "I never thought you were a spy, but it was a good excuse."

"For what?"

"For being with you, silly."

I feel better. I suppose I could put up with Lord Ludo and the rest. I say I'll consider it.

We take the train back and jump into Sybil's car to get to the meeting at Kams' house. "The less you say, the better our chances," she tells me, as though I'm a child who can't be trusted to behave itself.

We're ushered into Kams' dining room. She's sitting at the head of the table. Lord Ludo and Jack Stickler are on either side of her. Sybil sits down next to Ludo and motions me towards chairs lined up against a wall. Three other people are sitting there already.

Kams clears her throat. "Shall we begin? We have several candidates to interview today." She looks across at the four of us and summons Juniper, a tall, thin, redheaded woman.

"Now then, Juniper, why do you want to join our club?" Ludo demands.

"Because I'm good-hearted and I sincerely want the betterment of the planet and the improvement of language."

So far so good. "And how do you propose to accomplish this?" Kams asks.

"By setting words free. I'm a Liberationist. Let them run wild, scamper across the countryside and multiply like rabbits – or not, as they please."

Sybil smiles encouragingly, but Jack Stickler says, "No. Absolutely not! We must have control. Words should be overseen and properly presented."

"So that they may flourish, surely," Ludo says genially. He turns to Juniper, "Would you be interested in a project that involves teaching English to wildlife?"

"English to wildlife?" Juniper repeats wonderingly.

"Yes, take words to the countryside, spread them about. Teach the rabbits, the cows, the sheep, anyone who'll listen," Ludo says heartily. "You could work with Jack here or even with Kams."

"I'm not sure," Juniper replies. "I also believe in animal rights."

"Wonderful!" cries Kams. "That fits right in with biodiversity, animal welfare and salvaging the planet. We will work together. Let's teach the animals English so that they may participate in the affairs of men, and women, of course. You may join."

"They may not want to learn English," Sybil protests.

"Was that a 'No' vote?" Kams demands.

"Of course not," Sibyl says hastily.

"Fine!" Juniper is given a seat at the table.

"Next candidate," Kams barks.

An old man shuffles up and sits down facing the committee.

"Well?" Kams asks. "What's your name? Why do you wish to join us and what can you offer?"

No answer.

Jack Stickler intervenes. "I brought him along. He doesn't speak. I call him Sav as in Noble Savage."

"Where's he from?" asks Ludo.

"Could be from anywhere. He's probably English," Stickler replies. "He's an abolitionist, wants to abolish words because they're a means of oppression."

Sybil and Ludo are both appalled. "How can we possibly countenance such a thing?" Ludo begins.

Stickler interrupts him. "He'll do as he's told. I thought he could do the pruning for us, even zap when necessary."

"Well, if you'll take responsibility …" Sybil sounds doubtful. "Do you think you and Sav might consider locking up words rather than destroying them?"

"Certainly," says Stickler.

Juniper raises her hand. "If he doesn't speak, how do you know that's what he wants?"

"I interpret his silence," Stickler says confidently.

They're desperate for recruits, I realise, but should I join? Kams waves Sav to a seat at the table.

"Next recruit, I mean candidate," Kams calls.

A comfortable looking woman rises. She sits down at the table and introduces herself. "I'm Connie, short for conservative with a small 'c'. And I would very much like to join your club for The Welfare of the Planet and the Preservation of English."

Kams leans forward. "I, myself, am a conservationist, but I have a feeling we might work happily together. Did you have anything particular in mind?"

"Yes," replies Connie. "I'm keen on a campaign to make everyone speak the King's English. Australians, Canadians and other members of the Commonwealth will have to be re-educated, also Americans, and most especially Indians. Can't understand a word they're saying. And all the words should have the King's head on them. That will make it clear whose language it is!"

"Now then, Connie, one mustn't be racist," Ludo protests.

"I'm not being racist," Connie replies. "I'm being English." She sits back looking pleased with herself.

Stickler's excited. "D'you know," he says, "I'm working on a Test of English as a Native Language to replace TOEFL. Perhaps you could join me?"

"Delighted, I'm sure." She takes her seat next to Sybil.

It's my turn next, but Kams has other ideas. "Before we get to the next candidate, who has been sprung on us without notice, I would like to draw your attention to two other matters."

She points dramatically at a pot of cyclamens sitting on the table. "They are the problem."

Everyone stares at the cyclamens. They're a vivid pink, but they don't seem to be doing anything disruptive.

Satisfied with the effect, she addresses us, "The Greeks are demanding their cyclamens back. The plant has the same name today that it had in Ancient Greece. That's what Theophrastus called it. In fact, they want all their words back, and their stories. So do the Italians, so do the Israelis. So do the Indians, though they're mostly on about arithmetic. They're demanding the return of Arabic numerals which they say belong to them. And most of all they want 'zero'."

"If they want nothing, give them nothing," chortles Connie.

Kams ignores her. "Should they succeed, it's goodbye to computer science and to arithmetic."

Ludo frowns, then his brow clears. "Don't worry," he tells the others. "If they try anything, we'll charge them all extortionate fees."

"For what?" asks Sybil.

"For the use of English. It's like charging for a software licence. Accepted practice."

"And if they refuse?" asks Sybil.

"We'll accuse them of using pirated software," Ludo replies cheerfully.

Kams looks relieved. "I'll go on then to the second item. Some of the minority languages have clubbed together and are likening English to the Crown of Thorns starfish. They see themselves as the precious coral consumed by it."

"Don't worry," Stickler says in his forthright way. "We merely have to point out that that is not an acceptable simile. Words are not starfish."

"And in any case," Ludo says sagely, "there is nothing wrong with starfish per se. Suppose starfish ruled the world, would that be so bad?"

"We could speed up the process of the spread of English," Sybil offers, "with judicious alliances."

"What, marry off our words into foreign families?" Kams is indignant.

"Absolutely not!" Connie puts in.

I feel horribly uncomfortable. I find I agree with Kams and Connie. I don't want to agree with them about anything.

"Hybrids are hardy," Juniper mutters under her breath. Sybil represses a giggle. Kams looks around. My turn next? No, Kams has decided to break for sandwiches. They all get up and go to the sideboard. I stay where I am, not sure whether I'm entitled to sandwiches yet. Sybil joins me with a plateful of food and some wine.

"Sybil," I whisper, "I don't want to be a Glad-Hearted Gardener."

"Good-Hearted," she corrects. "They're all quite nice really. Don't you care about your mission? You'll need an organisation of like-minded people."

"They're not like-minded."

"Minds can be changed," she says smoothly. "Besides, don't you want to be with me?"

They're returning to the table, and before I know it I hear Kams calling, "The last candidate, Madam Demo. Is it Miss or Mrs?"

I rise slowly and sit down facing them. "Ah, Demo, do sit down." Lord Ludo, affable as ever. "I understand from Sybil that you're interested in liquefying language. I wonder, might you be the person I've been looking for?"

I hope not. He peers at me and carries on, "How shall I describe myself? I am an avant-garde reactionary. I want a return to Elizabethan English, to its fluidity, its inventiveness, its exuberance; but made new, of course. More – more liquid. I'm engaged in a translation of Shakespeare into modern slang; but the slang keeps mutating. What do you say? Will you help?"

Before I can reply, Sybil steps in. "Demo wants words to be more metamorphic, to contain in themselves the knowledge that they are born of time and describe a reality in which things change, one into another, as do the words themselves in an ocean of time – or something of the sort."

Ludo looks upon us benignly, Kams is suspicious, Sav impassive. Connie is looking to Ludo for a lead, and Juniper seems to be listening to some other noise. But Stickler's response is instant. "Are you suggesting that pronouns become a matter of choice, and that adjectives be turned into adverbs?"

"In the worst tradition of our best athletes," Sybil whispers.

"It has to be done judiciously," I reply.

"Exactly," agrees Ludo. "And each instance must be ruled upon by persons with experience and expertise."

"And who might they be?" Stickler demands.

"Us," Sybil tells him smiling.

I don't want Ludo taking me under his wing. I try to reassure Stickler. "When one liquefies language, there may be some liquidation, but I'm a maker as well, not an anarchist."

"No, but you might be a terrorist or a spy," Kams mutters darkly.

Sybil intervenes. "Demo is not an anarchist or a terrorist or a spy. The truth is —" She pauses to make them wait for the truth. "Demo is a poet, and therefore an individualist and therefore slippery!"

"Wonderful!" cries Ludo. "Someone after my own heart. You must join us immediately. Out of the old, we make the new. New lamps from old – the cry of poets down the centuries. Don't you agree, Demo?"

I nod feebly.

Kams turns on Sybil. "It's all very well you recommending Demo, but Sybil dear, you're liberal to the point of being a libertine. 'Come one, come all,' you say to the world, but Demo may have ulterior motives."

I've had enough. "Of course I have ulterior motives. It's called having an inner life. And I'm certainly not who I seem to be. I'm constantly changing. I am a metamorph!"

"Splendid!" cries Ludo, more enthusiastic than ever. "A metamorph! The very thing!"

Kams subsides; a few of the others nod, welcoming me to the gang. Sybil grins and winks at me. I'm in. But I'm not joining without a struggle.

"I have some doubts," I begin.

Ludo cuts me short. "Shall we save them for next time? Kams, will you make sure that our new cellmates – ha, ha – are put on the payroll immediately." He beams at us. I'm gobsmacked. I've become a Good-Hearted Gardener, and I'm going to be paid.

6

On remote shores whole lives are lived in English

A couple of days later Sybil and I pack a picnic basket and drive into the country. We settle under a willow and watch a mother duck persuading her ducklings into the water. I'm happy being with Sybil, looking at the river, munching a roll, sharing it with the ducks. Sybil says fondly, "Darling Demo, you're like the ducklings. You don't know what's good for you."

"You're good for me," I reply smiling.

"And so are the Good-Hearted Gardeners."

"Sybil," I protest, "I'm really not sure I want to be in the pay of MI5. Why do we have to be a secret agency?"

"In case people misconstrue our motives and think that though the Empire is gone, we're now engaged in an Empire of the Mind."

"Well, are we? If so, I don't condone it. I don't want to be colonised! And I don't want to colonise anybody. I resign," I tell Sybil indignantly.

"You can't be colonised," Sybil murmurs.

"Why not?" I demand.

"Because you have been already," she says sweetly.

Appalling, but true. I open my mouth and close it again. Sybil continues, "Don't you see, my darling, it's done and dusted. We're talking in English. We make love in English. We're bickering in English. And on remote shores whole lives are lived in English."

She pauses. "Is it so wrong then to care about what happens to English words with or without the King's head on them?" she asks smiling.

I smile back in spite of myself. But the problem remains. I think in English. I can't be expected to give up thinking. And I dream in English, no one can censor their dreams. I won't and I can't.

Aloud I say, "And we're funded by MI5?"

Sybil nods. "Each of us gets a generous stipend. It's for services rendered to the government."

This is getting worse and worse. "Come clean, Sybil. Is world domination our ultimate object?"

Sybil shrugs. "It makes sense. One Language. One World. Planetary Peace. Through Global Domination we could Save the Species and the Planet."

"And I, a product of imperialism, am supposed to collude in this? I quit. I abdicate. I resign. I do not want to be a Good-Hearted Gardener or a minion of anyone's empire."

Sybil takes a sip of wine. "No one is asking you to be a gardener or a minion. All we're talking about is planetary peace. No more war. No petty squabbling among rival nations. All for one and one for all! What's wrong with that?"

"What's wrong with it is that it sets up English at the expense of all other languages!"

"Wouldn't it be a good thing if everyone could speak to everyone else and actually understand what was being said?"

"A lot of the world does speak English and nobody understands what's being said," I retort.

"Connie would tell you that that is because they do not speak the King's English," Sybil replies laughing. "Which language would you like instead?"

"The language of trees."

"Trees?"

"Yes. They're so articulate. They look like dancers in slow time."

"Or the language of fish," Sybil offers. "Fish are so fluent and have so many fins – the dorsal, the pectoral, the pelvic, the caudal. Each flick expresses a shift in meaning, a nuance. In such a language there could be no misunderstandings."

"Or the misunderstanding could multiply. We'd have to spend a lot of time in the water," I object. "What about the language of birds instead? In addition to the swoop and glide and tilt of their wings to convey meaning, they chirrup and cheep and we can actually hear them."

Sybil likes the idea. "We could twitter and tweet, whistle and warble with the best of them."

Our mood lightens, but just then we see Juniper walking towards us. "As I pulled up at your house," she says awkwardly, "I saw you driving off, so I followed."

There's no help for it. Sybil motions her to a corner of the rug and offers her a roll and a glass of wine. Even though I'm irritated with Juniper for barging in on us, I like Sybil for being so nice. Sybil quells me with a glance, so I try to be nice as well.

Juniper begins at once. "The thing is I'm worried about joining the Society of Gardeners. Is the whole thing a right wing plot? I'm not right wing. I'm not sure I'm left wing either. I like rabbits, birds, fish … People are more difficult."

"We were just talking about using the language of trees or birds or fish," I tell her.

Juniper cheers up instantly. "That would be lovely!" she says. "And what about the languages of badgers and boars and bees and butterflies, and all the others?"

"Yes," I admit, "just to choose one language, say the language of birds, would be discriminatory."

"Oh birds don't have just one language," Juniper informs us. "It depends on who they are and where they live. Gulls have picked up a smattering of other languages from here and there because they migrate; but there must be over 9,000 bird languages, not to mention dialects. I understand two or three kinds of birds and the local rabbits. But there's a lot going on. I don't understand most of it."

I look at Juniper with new eyes. I'm impressed, though she clearly doesn't see herself as remarkable in the least.

Sybil nods. "And I suppose each kind of tree has a different language? How would we select?"

I want to question the supremacy of English. The trouble is, it's the only language I can really use. "Do you think you could write a poem in the language of fish?" I ask Sybil.

She hesitates. "Perhaps," she replies. "If I worked hard and after many years of practice."

That's what I was afraid of. I don't believe that I could master the stances of trees or achieve even minimal control over the murmuring of leaves. Besides, I haven't any leaves. It's disheartening.

Juniper hasn't any answers either. She has another misgiving. "If they start paying me, will I lose I lose my benefits?"

"What are you getting your benefits for?" Sybil asks.

"For being poor, I suppose," Juniper replies.

"Once you get the stipend, you won't be poor." Sybil pauses, then decides to tell us what she knows. "Ludo and I had a meeting with the bosses the other day. They wanted us to recruit. Well, we've done that. Now they want results. Ludo has had to see them again. I expect he'll call another meeting soon."

"How much is the stipend?" Juniper asks.

"£2000 a month to begin with, plus expenses if you are on an assignment," Sybil says.

Gobsmacked again. Juniper and I look at each other. Are we being asked to sell our souls? And should we go ahead and sell them? We're both quiet as we clear up the picnic and head home.

In the car I explain my difficulty to Sybil. "I can't help the British build another empire. And I certainly can't take money for doing so. It wouldn't be right. I've grown up thinking that getting rid of the British was a splendid thing."

"Darling Demo," Sybil replies, "nobody's asking you to build an empire. Perhaps all they want is world peace. And anyway, if you don't take the money, what are we going to live on?"

We! Live on! She's thinking about a future! For both of us! I'm so startled and so pleased that I can barely think.

Once back, Sybil tells me that she's going over to Kams' to study the goldfish in her pond. I nod. "I'll work in the garden, and listen to the blackbirds, also to the robins. I might record them."

Neither of us is confident that the languages of fish or of birds or of trees as world languages will actually serve. But if Juniper can learn some of these languages, perhaps we could too. I'm curious, and so is Sybil. What do fish say to one another? And the trees? Do they use blank verse or a different system?

I wander into the garden. Sybil drives off. In the evening over supper we report to each other how we got on. There are roses on her dining table. "We forgot about the language of flowers!" I exclaim.

Sybil demurs. "First we behead them, and then we expect them to convey a message. Better not go there. How did you get on with the garden birds?"

Should I tell her? Might as well. "I managed to make a really good recording of a young robin singing its heart out."

"Male or female?" Sybil interrupts.

"Male, I think."

"Go on."

"Well, then I played it back to the robin as a way to make a start. But the robin cocked his head and said to me in English, 'You do realise that that was an Ode to a Worm? Are you seriously telling me that there is nothing you would like better than a dish of worms?'"

"You're saying that robins understand English?"

I nod. "And who knows what else they understand. And the blackbirds as well. And the trees. Perhaps they've been eavesdropping on people all this time. How did you get on?"

"I sat by Kams' pond admiring the goldfish, their colours, and the way their fins moved in the water. After about half an hour I thought I was beginning to detect a pattern, when one of the fish swam close to the surface. It kept opening its mouth and closing it again. Puzzling. Eventually I realised it was talking to me. I tried lip-reading. It was saying three sentences over and over again: 'Please go away. You've gawped long enough. You're invading our privacy. Please ...' I got up immediately, of course."

"People don't know yet that robins and goldfish can speak English," I say thoughtfully.

"Perhaps everyone can speak English?" Sybil rejoins. "Well, there's a meeting tomorrow, Kams told me. We can talk about it then. "

I nod. I'm not at all sure I could express myself in whatever language goldfish speak, and I'd have to learn to lip read.

That night in bed, I ask Sybil whether she likes goldfish.

"Well, not yet, not particularly. But I might if I learnt their language. Do you like robins?"

"Not sure. Do you think goldfish and robins like us because they understand English?"

"I don't think so," she mutters, letting me burrow into her shoulder. "Go to sleep."

I lie there thinking about what difference it makes if goldfish speak English. I don't feel sleepy. In the end I get up and write a poem.

7

Fining babies

Once she's awake, I show Sybil my poem.

BEE ON ICE,
They say that in Japan little boys learn a Boy-Speak,
which is entirely different from little girl Girl-Speak.
And this would be extraordinary because Japan(ese?)
　　　　　　is extraordinary (and probably exotic)
until I start to think about it.

They say that in the north, the true and bitter north,
there are seventy different words for varieties of snow,
and – who knows? – seventy other words for varieties
　　　　　　　　　　　　　　of ice;
but in Hindi and Marathi, probably also
　　　　　　　　　in Telugu and Tamil,
one simple word
　　　　　　must suffice – for ice,
which would make us Indians niggardly,
　　　　　　　　　　　　were it not
for the fact that in the Perfect Language,
　　　　　　　　　(Sanskrit, naturally)

there are seventy different words
                    for the honey bee.
They say
        once it so happened a Sanskrit-speaking
                        Hindu
and a modern Inuit sat down to write
                    about a bee on ice.
And within the story
                the bee, of course, died,
but she died in icy splendour
                and is richly described.

And they say that when Siegfried tasted
                    the dragon's blood,
he straight off understood the language of birds.
That's not quite right.
What he understood
                was that birds do speak.
It's not hard.
A raised arm, a pat on the head
                are plain enough.
Cats and dogs, and birds as well —
                most living things —
have long understood human speech.
Let me paraphrase.
Servants understand a great deal of English,
and we who speak English, non-native English,
have a long understanding
                of a great deal of English,
and it has made us —
                well, some sort of English.
'Language is a means of communication'.
                        Yes!

'Language is a means of domination'.
                                        Oh yes!
But one day I will learn a million languages.
One day I will listen to the murmur of grass.
One day I will notice that each living thing,
                is shouting its tiny head off!

Sybil decides it would be a good way to start a discussion about birds and fish talking. At the meeting she gives everyone a copy of the poem. Juniper reads it and smiles. Kams sniffs. Sav looks at Stickler wanting to know whether to read it and gets told not to. Connie frowns and hunts for her glasses, and Ludo shoves it into his pocket.

For once he isn't beaming. "MI5 has given us an ultimatum," he says abruptly.

"Yes, Ludo," Sybil interjects, "but can't we at least look at the poem and talk about what we've just found out? It's important."

"This is no time for poetry or esoteric titbits. MI5 say they will stop our funding unless we give them more bang for their buck." Ludo almost scowls at her.

"'Bang for their buck'," Stickler mutters. "Is that English?"

"What do they want?" Kams inquires.

"They want us to monetise and weaponise." Ludo says this slowly and clearly so that we can take it in. "We're expected to come up with something useful. Begin brainstorming."

"Monetise and weaponise what?" Sybil asks.

"English."

We stare at Ludo and realise he's serious. We scratch our heads and think.

"How about persuading foreign students to come here and study all sorts of things in proper English?" Stickler suggests.

"Being done already. And we charge them quite a lot," Ludo replies.

"Increase the fees?" Connie offers.

"Difficult. Competition from the Americans, the Canadians and even the Australians. They've persuaded the world that they speak English."

"Set up branches of our universities in other countries and pull in the money?" Kams suggests.

"Being done already."

"Do that with the publishing houses?" Stickler says.

"Done already," Ludo repeats.

"Broadcast in English to the world at large and get advertising?" Connie puts in.

"Being done already," Ludo says. "They want us to think of something new."

"Agree to teach English in the Devanagari script?" This is from Sybil. I glance at her quickly. Is she serious?

"Or in ideogrammatic Chinese," I throw in.

"Wouldn't make money." Connie is dismissive.

"Is monetise the same as weaponise?" Juniper wants to know.

"Can be," Ludo replies. "Money buys things. Weapons make money."

"What about charging for the use of English?" Stickler asks.

"Can't enforce."

"Then a UN resolution that in the interests of World Peace everyone must learn at least two languages of which one must be English?" Stickler persists.

"In many countries that's being done already. It's just us – we tend to speak only English," Ludo replies.

"We could fine people for mistakes in spelling?" Kams suggests.

"And in grammar," Stickler adds.

"We'd have to fine ourselves," Ludo points out. "And there aren't many people left who could spot the mistakes. Besides, I think the bosses would prefer foreign money."

"Tax foreign names," I say suddenly. What am I saying? I'll get taxed.

"Brilliant!" says Connie. "Any name that has not been given to a British baby at least once should require a licence fee."

"Would that affect adults or only babies?" Sybil asks.

"Would it apply to pets?" Kams demands.

"At least it would deter immigrants," Connie interjects.

"Fine women for changing their names when they marry?" Juniper murmurs.

"There's already a fee for getting married. This could be an additional fee," Ludo replies.

"Could we charge for admitting foreign words into our dictionaries?" Sybil wonders. "Decide which words are legitimate like the French Academy?"

"They'd probably try to charge us for borrowing them," Ludo tells her. "So far all we've come up with is fining babies and charging women for getting married." He looks down-hearted.

Connie gives him a sympathetic smile. She says brightly, "Well, let's see what we can do to weaponise English."

Sav looks at Stickler. Stickler translates. "He says he is an accomplished arsonist and could set fire to foreign libraries."

Sybil turns pale. Ludo is shocked. Even Kams and Connie look horrified.

"What good would that do?" Kams demands.

"If we destroyed other people's words, they'd have to use ours and they'd need our help for which we could charge money," Stickler explains.

"No. No violence," Ludo says firmly.

"Lies are a weapon," Kams offers thoughtfully. "We could alter history, re-write the text books, generate fake news, mistranslate texts, put in adverts, control the media, change reality. Won't that do?"

"Being …" Ludo begins.

"Done already," the rest of us finish for him.

Connie makes a last effort. "The government could decree that one pound is now equal to ten. No need to bother with printing money. It would make everyone ten times as rich."

"Or ten times as poor," Stickler points out. "Everyone would get only a tenth of what they'd been getting."

We've run out of ideas. Kams produces sandwiches, which we nibble gloomily.

We've tried to think of something, and it has made us miserable. Stickler might want to punish people for committing solecisms, but I think he'd be happier paying them not to. Ludo just wants to rewrite Shakespeare in order to make the poetry intelligible. Connie wants to do whatever she thinks Ludo would approve of. And Kams is unsure whether any of this conserves anything. I have a feeling we're ashamed of ourselves for even trying to think of ways to monetise, weaponise, bowdlerise or do whatever it is the bosses want. I'm about to say so, when Juniper says softly, "There's a way out. We know something that might be useful. With help we could still achieve the betterment of language and the salvation of the planet. I'm not sure about being paid for it though."

"What are you talking about?" Ludo is incredulous.

"What we were trying to tell you right at the beginning," Sybil answers. "The birds and the beasts and most of the trees understand English."

"I knew it!" cries Connie looking smug. Stickler and Kams frown, trying to decide whether it's true, and whether it's a good thing.

"Are you quite sure?" Ludo asks.

"Reasonably sure," Sybil replies.

"Well! Then we have billions and zillions of spies!" Ludo exults.

"No!" Sybil, Juniper and I protest. "Zillions of fellow creatures to help save the planet."

"Oh, all right." Ludo shrugs. "If you think they might not co-operate otherwise. Have you spoken to any birds or fish or trees lately?"

Sybil tells the others about her encounter with the goldfish. She looks at me, so I have to tell them about the robin.

"They're not especially friendly, are they?" mutters Kams.

"They have no reason to be," Juniper says gently. "As a species we have a lot to answer for."

"But you've managed to learn four or five languages," I say to Juniper.

"How does one go about it?" Kams asks earnestly.

We hang on Juniper's words. "The first thing to do is to listen. Demo and Sybil were right to try that. But we have to be respectful, ask permission first. If you were a goldfish trapped in a goldfish pond, you wouldn't like being gawped at or eavesdropped upon. Or if you were a robin, you wouldn't like your song recorded without so much as an 'If you please'."

She's right. We're all quiet. We don't want to interrupt her, but when she says nothing more, Ludo asks, "Are you saying that we have to learn their language first? Otherwise they won't speak to us?"

"At least, it shows willing," Juniper replies. "We've killed them and eaten them or killed them for fun and not eaten them. We've caged them, exploited them and taken over their habitat so that they have nowhere to live. We can't expect to be liked."

"You're saying they understand English. Are they any good at it or is it just pidgin English?" Connie demands.

"Well, they're better at it than I am at their languages," Juniper replies. She pulls out a piece of paper from her pocket. "Here's poem a blackbird gave me. I'll read it, shall I?"

> *The blackbird sang her song.*
> > *The female doesn't sing?*
> *She sang anyway.*
> > *The garden was scruffy.*
> *Birds don't care?*
> > *She cared anyway.*
> *And the rain rained down, ran off*
> > *her back*
> *down the sleek feathers.*
> > *Birds don't —?*
> *Yes, they do. They feel the cold.*
> > *Sometimes the garden*
> > *leaves them desolate.*

"It's quite good," I mutter. "Is your friend telling us to shut up?"

"No," Juniper answers. "I think she's just singing about feeling cold."

We take that in. Everyone looks chastened, but we're also feeling much better. This is something we good-hearted gardeners feel more comfortable with, even though we're not quite sure how to proceed. We wander into Kams' garden. We're careful. We stay away from the pond, and try not to disturb the finches and tits. They're pecking away at a peanut feeder on a small rowan tree.

Everything feels different now that we know that the air is filled with millions of voices. I see Sav smile for the first time. Kams is thoughtful. She turns to Juniper and asks, "Owls or goldfish? A barn owl has settled in the ash tree at the bottom of my garden. Should I try to make friends with the owl first or with the goldfish?"

Juniper considers. "Owls aren't sociable, but for the sake of the planet, being on speaking terms with an owl would be very worthwhile. They have special powers."

"Such as?" I demand.

"They can see what's in front of them as well as what's behind them – they can swivel their heads right around. Some people think this means that they can see the future as clearly as the past. They have silent flight. You can't hear the swish of feathers when they swoop down. And they have nocturnal vision. To them whatever's hidden is as plain as daylight." She smiles at Kams. "It would mean late nights, but it's worth a try."

"I have trouble sleeping anyway," Kams replies. "What should I say to the owl?"

"Ask for advice."

"Why?"

"Well, we need it. And they're used to being asked for it."

I glance at Sybil and mutter, "We were also thinking of talking to birds. Would that be all right?"

"Of course," Juniper replies. "Birds would probably be best to start with. You could try eagles. Great eyesight. But they're hard to reach and used to doing what they like. Gulls, perhaps, because they travel. And crows. Crows aren't migratory, of course, but they're clever and they get about. If we could win over the crows, they could help us with everyone else. Do you think you and Sybil could talk to crows?"

"Love to," says Sybil happily, "if they'll talk to us."

"And there are gulls about. I could try talking to them," Ludo says.

"Sav and I could help," Jack Stickler offers.

"I could too," Connie adds. "Or I could help Kams if she'll have me. We could take turns staying up all night."

"That would be excellent." Kams is encouraging. I have to admit that when Kams is being nice, she is quite nice.

"Should we all meet in a week to tell each other how we got on?" Ludo asks.

We agree and turn to Juniper. We need her help. "Please Juniper, will you help?" Jack asks for all of us.

"Of course I will." She smiles, and suddenly it all seems possible.

"How should we begin?" Ludo asks anxiously.

"By sitting still."

Sav immediately plonks himself down cross-legged on the grass. He looks comfortable. The rest of us follow suit as best we can.

"And then?"

"Be quiet."

"And then?" whispers Ludo.

"Extend a peace offering?"

"What?"

"Food usually."

"And then?"

"Wait."

"And then."

"Wait some more."

We sit more or less quietly for nearly an hour.

"Now what should we do?" Ludo asks.

"Now, open your eyes and say 'Hello' very softly."

Ludo does so, and the tits and the finches, who are all lined up on a branch of the rowan tree, titter at us. It's a start. I don't mind being laughed at for the sake of such an adventure! Think of what we might learn! Not just English, but language itself might burst right open – the stances, the nuances, the multiple identities; tenses that belong to different periods; nouns that fluctuate according to the speaker. Sybil tries to calm me down, but I can tell that she is exhilarated.

As we head home I can hear crows. I'm getting sensitised.

8

Bad things happen in fairy tales

That evening we work hard. Sybil has instructed me to write a flattering poem about a crow, or a fable in which the crow comes off best. She's researching what they like to eat, their habits and habitats, their peculiarities. I've moved in with Sybil. We're not sure we're making a commitment, but living together will be cheaper. We're all going to have to think about how to manage. Sybil has her job at the dictionary project. I can always teach a course or two. Jack has an independent income. So has Kams. Ludo is quite rich. Juniper has her benefits, and probably Sav has as well. I'm not sure about Connie, but I don't think she's poor. I have a feeling that with the help of most of the other species we might save the planet, but I don't think MI5 will pay for it.

Sybil has been scouring the internet. I kiss the top of her head. She says I can't have any kisses until I've produced a poem.

"Why?" I demand. "Do you think a poem will help?"

"Don't know," Sybil replies. "But Juniper let drop that the only thing they like about us is our stories and poems – the ones in which they figure as heroes."

I sit down and try. It's not always possible to come up with something.

"In the crow family there are common crows, hooded crows, jays, magpies, choughs, daws, rooks, ravens and many more species the world over," she complains wearily.

"Let's stick with the common or carrion crow," I tell her. "That's the one we're likely to meet. I don't know if this fable will do." I offer her an old one.

"Read it," she commands.

I read aloud.

VIHAAN AND THE CROW

The crow looked at Vihaan. 'I,' said the crow, 'am more beautiful than the wells of sullen darkness at the rim of the universe. But you, Little One, wouldn't understand that. Your mind is a blank, a field of snow. I could walk across it and leave cuneiform marks, and you wouldn't even be able to read what had happened. And yet, I would find it worthwhile to know exactly what I look like to you, and when the sound of my voice impinges on your ears, what, if anything, you understand.'

Vihaan looked at the crow. Though only a baby he knew about colours, and he knew about light, but Lack Light on the windowsill was like nothing he had ever come across. Out of something Lack Light had made nothing. He had cut out light and he had cut out colour and out of the cut-outs he had made a shape that talked at him. Vihaan stretched out a friendly hand.

The crow flounced. Vihaan crowed. He liked what had happened. 'Listen,' instructed the crow. 'I am not nothing and I am not Lack Lustre. Look harder. I am subtle, I am shaded. I have texture and tone. And my black eyes shine without the aid of external light. I am wonderful!'

This last sentence was punctuated with such a loud squawk that Vihaan squawked back. The crow was startled. Had Vihaan uttered an arcane word?

'Listen,' said the crow. 'You are, perhaps, capable of more than I had thought. Let us be friends.'

Vihaan gurgled. And that is how it came about that the crow learnt to listen, and Vihaan learnt to talk.

I wait for Sybil's response. She hesitates. "*'Wells of sullen darkness at the rim of the universe'* are all very well, but the fable isn't altogether flattering to crows."

"Oh, it will do," says a baritone voice through the open window. "Just change the last sentence."

We peer out. Can't see anything. "Is that you, Crow? Signor Crow? How should we address you?" asks Sybil.

"Yes, it's me. Just call me Corvo. Here, I'll dictate. The last sentence should go: *'And that is how it came about that the crow taught Vihaan both to talk and to listen.'* I'll submit it to the archive. They'll probably accept it. See you at breakfast tomorrow. Fried eggs and bacon?"

Sybil and I stare at each other. First contact! Corvo has deigned to talk to us. We put together a bit of food, gobble it up, set the alarm and fall into bed, hardly able to believe our luck.

That night we are especially gentle and loving with each other. "Happy?" she asks.

"Yes," I reply. "To be at peace with the world, with everyone and everything – it feels wonderful." She snuggles closer.

"Everything isn't necessarily benign," she murmurs.

"That's true," I agree. "Bad things happen in fairy tales." Nevertheless we sleep well that night.

The next morning, I jump out of bed. Bacon and eggs, he had said. I set three places, open the window and start frying bacon. Does he eat toast? Does he really want me to call him Corvo? I decide to be exceedingly polite and careful.

As I'm about to butter the toast, Corvo flies in and takes his place on the table. He nods by way of saying 'Good Morning'.

After he's finished two rashers of bacon, one egg and half a piece of toast, he's ready for conversation. "Got anything else?" he asks cheerfully.

"More bacon?" asks Sybil.

"No, no. More poems. We like poems except when you use unpleasant similes, or give unforgivable meanings to words like 'bestial', 'beastly' and even 'animal'."

Sybil looks at me. I haven't come up with a poem. "Well, I have one," she says diffidently, "but it depicts a crow in manipulative mode."

"Manipulative is good. We pride ourselves on being wily birds. Let's have the poem." Sybil reads:

I AM CROW
Crow, crying in the wilderness,
*   while embarrassed onlookers*
are forced to watch, says that she
*   is a solitary bird*
and belonging, as she does to a group of one,
*   needs no one,*
but her wing is broken, and do we seriously mean
*   to do nothing at all?*
She hobbles a little, one wing trailing.
*   At last, a kind woman*
rushes up. Crow triumphant!
*   She hops on her shoulders,*
digs in her claws, and makes her carry her,
*   till she gets bored.*
Then she hops off.

'I am Crow.
        My wing is broken.
                Do you seriously mean …?'

"Brava!" cries Corvo, flapping his wings and knocking over Sybil's mug. "We won that round. The Queen will like this one."

While Sybil is mopping up her coffee, I ask Crow, "Venerable Sir, do we figure at all in your stories and poems?"

He blinks and appears slightly embarrassed. "You do figure now and then, but only as giants and ogres and fiends from hell whom heroic crows contrive to kill or dupe somehow." He shrugs. "No offence. It's just how it is. And you don't have to be so damn polite. I'm just an ordinary creature – like you."

"We thought —" Sybil begins lamely.

"You thought now that you've discovered our creature-hood, you ought to treat us with the utmost respect, put us on a pedestal and venerate us. The point is not that we are particularly meritorious; the point is that we *are*. Stop kowtowing. We don't want to become extinct along with you. Let's do our best to work together and prevent that if we possibly can."

While Sybil and I take that in, Corvo finishes the rest of the bacon.

"So you know why we've come to you for help?" I ask Corvo.

"Of course."

They consider us important enough to eavesdrop on. I hadn't thought that the Good-Hearted Gardeners were of such consequence. I look gratified and Corvo sees this. "It's not that you're particularly important or particularly good-hearted, it's just that it's the first time any of you has asked us for help."

Sybil and I look suitably abashed.

"Look, before your audience with our Queen today, you'll

have to acquire some crow speech and have some idea of how to behave."

"What is your Queen called?" Sybil asks.

"She has taken the title Queen of the Night – she likes Mozart – and enjoys being addressed as Serenissima on the grounds that she never loses her cool. Now then, start cawing."

We try. Gradually, we improve. He tells us, "If you practise cawing up and down the scale all afternoon, you should be all right. The Queen will see you today at 6 p.m. under the copper beech beside the crooked bridge. Bring Juniper with you. She knows the protocol."

After he has flown out through the window, I turn to Sybil, "Do you think cawing at short notice is strictly necessary or is he just having a joke at our expense?"

"Oh, I think he means it," Sybil replies. "If we get a note wrong, the Queen will refuse to speak to us. I'm going to phone Juniper to ask how the others are getting on and to see if she'll come to tea before the audience."

I wander into the garden and nod politely at a robin sitting nearby.

"Demo," I hear Sybil call. "Come back and practise. Oh and we have to try to write something to please the Queen, at least a few lines."

I'm not sure I can caw and write at the same time. "Shouldn't we be trying to save the planet?" I complain.

"That too," Sybil replies.

We caw and we scribble, we scribble and caw. Our joint effort is a haiku:

The dapper crow perched
on a bird bath, sees herself
and is well content.

We're not sure it will do, but Sybil puts it in her pocket just in case.

9

They're good at it.
We are not.

When she arrives, Juniper tells us that Kams and Connie have made a tiny bit of progress with the barn owl. She has accepted their offering of shepherd's pie, and has told them that her name is Emma. Tonight, they're going to try bacon and liver and tomorrow an ordinary sausage with bits of chorizo in case she would like something spicy; if that works, the day after they'll offer a full-blown curry. It's slow going, but Juniper says that with owls one has to be careful. It occurs to me that Corvo scoffed his bacon happily and Emma ate up her shepherd's pie, but surely the pigs and the sheep would find this difficult? Can all the species co-operate? Perhaps when we get to know Corvo better, we could ask him about it.

Juniper, Sybil and I take a shortcut to the crooked bridge. It's a pleasant evening. There's a light breeze. Everything smells of summer and mown grass. Serenissima has already taken her place on the giant beech. Corvo is perched just behind her, and fifty more crows have arranged themselves on the other branches. They look magnificent.

I don't know whether we're expected to curtsey. I compromise by bowing from the waist and doing a namaskar.

I'm not sure what Sybil and Juniper do.

"You may present your gift," Corvo informs us.

Sybil fishes out the crumpled haiku and gives it to Corvo. He stands on one foot and presents it to the Queen. She glances at it and nods.

"It is acceptable," Corvo says. "Caw three times and state what you want."

All three of us caw in greeting, then switch into English. Juniper speaks for us, "O Serenissima, the planet is in danger. We need your help."

"And that's our problem too," the Queen replies graciously. "To start with here's a list of necessary measures. Write them down."

I pull out a scribble pad and a pen hastily. Corvo dictates.

~ *Abolish private property, so that cows can roam where they like, and not get eaten and not emit a noxious gas.*
~ *Set limits on the rights of any species to multiply freely, especially humans.*
~ *Make specific areas of the planet off limits to species which don't already live there, for example, the bottom of the ocean, the Amazon forest and the polar ice caps.*
~ *Set up reservations for other species free of humans.*

"Sorry, the other way about."

~ *Set up reservations to which humans must confine themselves.*

"Oh and

~ *Make wilful pollution a capital crime.*

"Slow down, Corvo," I plead. "Anything else?" I ask after I've jotted that down.

"Yes," says the Queen. She dictates.

~ Biodiversity is needful. Do not kill off other animals.
~ Avoid eating meat. It harms the planet.
~ And 'Learn of the green world'.

She's quoting Pound! I'm so startled I don't say another word. Sybil speaks up. "We thank you, Serenissima. But how are we to enforce these measures?"

"For that," says Serenissima grandly, "you must consult the owls. We will help. Corvo will be our liaison."

I do my respectful namaskar. Sybil attempts a quick bob. Later I ask Juniper what she usually does, and she says she just waves and smiles and says goodbye. "They're suspicious of any reverential stuff," she explains, "They say it's like men calling women their better halves, but depriving them of real power."

Our encounter with the Queen of the Night hasn't gone too badly. We return home and Juniper rings up Kams, who sounds sleepy. She must have taken to sleeping by day and waking at night. Juniper tells her what The Queen of the Night said, and Kams says to come over by ten that night for Emma's dinner, though she might want it later than that.

We grab some supper. "Does Emma require a poem as well?" I ask anxiously.

Juniper shakes her head. "No. The less we say the better. She doesn't like listening to other people talk."

"No flattery? No elaborate greeting? No long-winded titles?" Sybil wants to know.

"No. She'll cut you short. Just get to the point. Be as succinct as possible."

"Doesn't she have any good points?" I demand.

"She doesn't think that not wanting to be friends with us is a bad point," Juniper replies. Having done her best to show us our place in relation to owls, Juniper leaves. She'll meet us at Kams', and meanwhile, she says, she'll try to find out how Ludo and the others have got on.

"I can't believe Emma isn't susceptible to flattery. Everyone is," I say to Sybil.

"Yes, but perhaps not from us," Sybil points out.

"Well, a quote from Shakespeare then, just in case." I hunt on the internet, but find that all the references are dark. Who knows, perhaps Emma might like that, but best to leave it. At ten o'clock we arrive at Kams' and ring the bell. The moon is almost full and there's enough light to see by. Sybil looks beautiful by moonlight, which is a cliché I know, but clichés are truthful sometimes. I kiss her hair and she says, "Shush, concentrate on the job." I am concentrating on the job. Life is worth living and I very much want the planet to survive. Juniper joins us. And Kams and Connie emerge laden with blankets, folding chairs and tonight's offering. We help carry things to the bottom of the garden and settle ourselves. To pass the time I ask about Emma's likes and dislikes. I'm instantly hushed.

"Speak when you're spoken to," Connie whispers. "That's Emma's rule."

After an hour or so of sitting still, Sybil and I stretch our legs. "Did you write anything?" she asks softly. "I tried a limerick," I reply, "but look at the words that rhyme with owl – howl, scowl, growl, foul, prowl, yowl. I don't think it would have been appreciated."

We return to find that Emma has emerged. She utters one word, "Dinner." Kams and Connie scurry forward and serve it to her in a silver dish on a snow white napkin.

After she has finished eating, Emma speaks again. "The Crow Queen has acquainted me with the manifesto she has worked out for you. It will suffice. What is your problem?"

I notice Corvo has appeared unobtrusively and is sitting at a respectful distance on a nearby bough.

Juniper steps forward. "How to enforce it?" she says briefly.

"Threaten them," says Emma.

"They are already threatened," Corvo tells her soberly. "We all are. But they are singularly brainless. Total destruction doesn't focus their minds."

"In that case, let all life on earth turn against them. That will leave them with no choice," Emma pronounces.

The prospect of gulls diving at us, tigers attacking us, insects biting us, so appals Sybil that she bursts out before she can stop herself. "Please Madame Emma, we're not all bad!"

"Your morals are irrelevant," Emma replies coldly.

"Then why single us out?"

Sybil is in danger of annoying Emma. Corvo intervenes smoothly, "We are not discussing the questionable practices of diverse species – male polar bears sometimes eat their cubs, certain spiders devour their mates – not nice. What we are concerned with is which species does the most harm. You stand out."

Emma blinks at us disdainfully and turns to Corvo. "Inform the other species and send out gulls to broadcast the plan. To get you going here are some suggestions:

Stage One: Passive Resistance
- *Pigs to go on hunger strike.*
- *Horses to refuse to race, cats to stop purring and dogs to consistently disobey orders.*
- *Sheep and goats to wander where they like.*

At this point Corvo interrupts her respectfully. "Madame Emma, it might be best to leave out the cats and dogs. They'll be conflicted. Some of them actually love their so-called owners."

"Very well," Emma continues, "but make the importance of passive resistance quite clear. Hens, for example, must not lay eggs, or, at least, not lay them where they might be found.

The Next Stage: Proactive Measures
~ Birds to shit on people and on motor cars whenever possible.
~ Whales to overturn fishing trawlers.
~ Rats and mice to chew through cables.
~ And large herd animals to stampede through the countryside
*   and destroy whatever impedes their progress.*

"And the Big Beasts, Madame, should they be deployed?" Kams asks deferentially.

"The pachyderms and the big cats? No, they'd get shot down. Tell them to stay put. An occasional trumpet or a growl or a roar will be contribution enough."

"Will we need Stage Three?" asks Juniper quietly.

"It may come to that." Emma is nothing if not fierce and thorough.

Stage Three: Open Warfare
~ Aerial Attacks to be launched with the help of hornets
*   and wasps. Senior posts to be held by eagles and condors.*
*   At that point they will certainly help.*
~ Marines to be organised by dolphins and seals.
~ And Artillery to be deployed under the generalship of ants.
~ Gulls to supply a Messenger Service, as well as Intelligence.

"You, Juniper, are to be the Field Marshall or the Generalissima or whatever title you like. You have overall charge."

Juniper is appalled. "Oh no, Emma. I couldn't kill anyone. I don't think I could even give the order."

Emma focuses on her with her round owl eyes. "That's precisely why I'm putting you in charge. War should be avoided if at all possible. They're good at it. We are not. Moreover you are a linguist. Communication is supremely important. Drop flyers. Deluge the internet, and recruit all sympathetic humans."

"May we report to you, Madame Emma?" Connie asks humbly.

"You may. Come tomorrow with a red hot curry. I would like to taste it just once. Should it be necessary, Corvo here will keep me informed. Now go. I want the rest of the night to myself." Then she relents. "I will help."

Corvo takes off. The rest of us, overwhelmed by Emma's Master Plan, thank her and creep away.

10

If the horses co-operated

Sybil and I fall into a dead sleep when we get back and are still fast asleep when the phone rings at nine in the morning. It's Ludo for Sybil. He says it's urgent, so I make coffee and put breakfast together. Juniper has told Ludo about the Manifesto and the Master Plan. And, for their part, Ludo and the others have made friends with a gull called Gulliver. Ludo wants to know if they could please come with Gulliver to Sybil's garden at three o'clock, and would we inform Kams and Connie? And meanwhile, would we prepare drafts of the Manifesto and Master Plan to drop as flyers from the sky above? And, as Jack is working on various forms of messaging to spread across the internet, would we send him copies of the drafts? We take in all that and get to work right away. Just then, a robin hops onto the breakfast table.

"Could I have a piece of bread and butter please? I see you're working on the flyers. I'll help."

"How did you know?" I ask, as I set down a plate of buttered bread in front of her.

"Word gets about," she replies. "Do you think I might have a bit of sugar please?"

I sprinkle some sugar on her bread. She eats. We work. After a while she says, "Make sure the flyers are light so that they're easy to carry and so that the wind will broadcast them. Everyone wants to help. For smaller birds you might want smaller sizes. Oh, and make sure you use recycled paper."

Sybil nods. She has given the Manifesto a bright pink background and the Master Plan a bright blue one.

Once we've got the drafts ready, and the robin has eaten half her bread and flown away with the other half, we walk down to the bakery. By the time we get back, make sandwiches and start setting out chairs it's almost two thirty.

"I wonder why the gull is called Gulliver," I say idly as I bring yet another chair into the garden.

"It's a good name, isn't it?" A voice replies. A large herring gull is perched on the fence. He goes on cheerfully, "I chose it myself. Like Gulliver I travel to far away countries, make up tales about what happens there, and enjoy watching people try to convince themselves that the stories have nothing to do with them. Irony, you see. I'm an admirer of *The Travels.*"

Sybil and I are taken aback, but we nod and smile nicely. Gulliver says, "I'm early, but I was peckish. May I sit at the table please?"

"Of course," Sybil replies.

Gulliver swoops down on the table and walks about inspecting the sandwiches. "Chutney, tomato, cheese, cucumber," he mutters. "Ah I see you've got some crab! Excellent. Anything else?" He nibbles at a crab sandwich as unobtrusively as possible.

"Well, there's cake," Sybil offers.

"No, no. There are other kinds of sustenance," he tells her. "Crows aren't the only one who like poetry. You wouldn't happen to have a poem or two about gulls by any chance?"

"Well, as a matter of fact …" Sybil produces a scrap of paper. She has written a limerick. Whew!

"Read it," commands the gull.

Sybil reads.

There was once a gull called Gulliver
Who was especially helpful and clever.
Set him a task.
You just had to ask.
He would never fail to deliver.

"Excellent! How did you know I was helpful and clever? That was very perspicacious of you. You are a charming woman. Perhaps we could be friends?"

Sybil merely says, "We are friends. We're all on the same side."

Just then Corvo arrives. He nods to Gulliver and shows me a sheet of paper with a drawing on it. "It's a pack we designed for the flyers. It can be made in different sizes and strapped on the back. The bird carrying it tugs a ribbon dangling in front and all the leaflets flutter down."

"Isn't there some danger of exposing our plans?" Sybil asks.

Corvo shrugs. "We have to keep those on our side informed. Besides, with any luck, the governments of the world won't take us seriously until we're well advanced. We'll need to put in an order for the flyers and packs. There was some objection to using so much paper, so some of the trees have agreed to supply us with suitable leaves."

I nod. What else can I do? Not only are we not going to be paid by MI5, there are going to be expenses. We'll have to raise money. Just then Corvo notices the crab sandwiches, hops on the table, and pushes Gulliver aside. There's a flapping of wings. I manage to separate them before they knock everything over. I divide the sandwiches, give them a plate each and go inside to make more. Meanwhile Ludo, Jack, Sav, Connie and Kams arrive. We settle down, Gulliver on the arm of Ludo's chair, Corvo on the arm of Sybil's. At first we all talk and eat and tell each other what we've been doing. It turns out that Jack and Ludo didn't get far with the black-headed gulls. They were too timid, but then Sav came across Gulliver squawking loudly from a chimney top, and once they'd made friends, their problems were solved, well, very nearly solved.

"I'll take care of logistics with Ludo's help," Gulliver says. "We can distribute flyers all over the countryside in his motor car. My fellow gulls and some of the other migrants can take packages abroad. And some can be given to the smaller birds to distribute here."

"Agreed," says Ludo.

"And I could do the digital stuff," Jack offers. "I'm good with computers and I have super swift broadband, but I could use some help."

"I will help," declares Kams, coming to his aid like a battle cruiser, and that settles that.

"And we'll need someone to liaise with organisations that are sympathetic to us: Third Rock, Genesis, Live Green, Oxygenators, Bee Friends and so forth," Sybil murmurs.

"I can do that with Sav's help," Juniper says. "I'm already a member of most of them. And so is Sav."

We all look at Sav. He offers one word, "Yes."

"How do you propose to fund all this?" Corvo asks soberly.

"You could steal some money." Gulliver is being snide. "You and the magpies are good at that."

"I could," retorts Corvo, "but a pound at a time wouldn't get us anywhere. We need thousands, hundreds of thousands, millions."

This silences us all as we try to think where we might get millions, then Corvo says. "Stealing information, which we can turn into money, will be easier and more profitable than stealing money." He turns to Gulliver. "You hear a great deal of gossip as you fly here and there."

"And you lot," Gulliver says to Corvo, "are ubiquitous. You could pick up anything from anywhere – from banks, racing stables, stock exchanges, casinos, especially from places where piles of money swish around."

"Yes," mutters Corvo thoughtfully. "Yes, we could." "Would you," he asks Sybil and me, "be the receivers? For information only, not for goods," he adds hastily.

"Of course," Sybil says. "But what would we do with it?"

"I know what to do with it." Connie speaks with huge confidence. "I used to be an investment banker. Just keep the info coming, I'll do the rest."

We breathe a sigh of relief and look at Connie with admiration. "Who would have thought that the Glad-Hearted Gardeners had so much talent?" I murmur happily.

"Good-Hearted," Sybil corrects.

We smile at one another and relax a little. "I wish Emma could know how well we're getting on," Kams says.

"She knows," Corvo tells her. "I've been keeping her informed."

"Did she say anything?" Sybil asks.

"Three words," Corvo replies. "Prepare for chaos."

Juniper calls the meeting to order. Even the songbirds are relatively quiet. They want to listen in. Well, there's no harm in that.

"Emma is right," Juniper says soberly. "At first there will be chaos. To minimise it, we'll have to organise rapidly and start as soon as possible. We're in the middle of June. Shall we say that Stage One, Passive Resistance, begins on the First of July?"

We agree, but I think we're all feeling dazed, and not at all sure how we metamorphosed from good-hearted gardeners into revolutionaries. Perhaps good-hearted people are revolution-aries? The potential is there.

"Priorities?" Juniper asks.

"Funds," Connie says at once. "Corvo, can you arrange to have the crows spy on the Bank of England? The Monetary Policy Committee has its monthly meeting the day after tomor-row. If interest rates go up, the pound will rise. I can make money on Forex with that, but I need to know in advance."

"No problem!" Corvo replies. The blackbirds crowd around him. They want to help. They offer to spy on No. 10 and No. 11 Downing Street. They have backyard friends.

"Next, here are the names of the six richest men in the whole world. Whatever they invest in, we follow suit. This requires instant communication across continents. We need contacts. Sav, Juniper, can you reach the branches of sympathetic organisations, and convey a message from Gulliver to set up surveillance? And Jack can you set up links that can't be hacked?" Connie looks like a different woman, no longer fluffy and bossy – more like a virtuoso about to give a command performance. She's enjoying herself.

Juniper and Sav nod, Jack says, "Yes," and Gulliver says he'll record a message at once. Then he turns to the sparrows perched on the fence and asks nicely if they'll put in a word as well. After all, sparrows have connections all over the world. The sparrows tell him they would be delighted.

"And finally," Connie continues, "we need money to make money. I'll put in fifty thousand."

"I'll put in another fifty," Ludo says. The rest of us put in what we can.

"And now," says Juniper, "we must organise ourselves."

"You are the Commander-in-Chief," Kams tells her. "Tell us who is to do what."

"I'm only in charge until the planet is stabilised and our species is curbed," Juniper replies. "Right. Here's the set up. I'm the PM, Sav is the Deputy PM, Connie's The Chancellor, Ludo and Gulliver are Joint Foreign Secretary, Demo and Corvo are Joint Defence Secretary, Jack is in charge of Communications, Sybil is the Cultural Secretary and will take care of propaganda, and Kams is the Home Secretary. Kams will consult Emma and together with Jack and Corvo as Heads of Intelligence, they'll run the spy network, guard against opposition and keep Demo informed should hostilities break out." My heart quails. I do not want to be Defence Secretary; I do not want to send out troops. But I don't know how to refuse.

Juniper sees the look on my face and says gently, "We'll all do our best to avoid Stage Three and outright war. Similar cabinets will be set up all over the world with a friendly organisation at their core. For example, Third Rock are based in LA, Live Green in New Delhi, The Oxygenators in Geneva and so forth."

Two robins descend on the table. They puff out their breasts. "If there should be war," they say to me seriously, "we robins will be your vanguard."

I look at the little redbreasts. They sense my disbelief and continue, "Don't you see, when the enemy troops see a bunch of robins, they'll put down their guns. They'll think it's not manly to shoot robins – at least not in Britain. They think we're cute. We're not really. We can be quite bellicose, but they don't know that."

I don't know what to say to them, and so I say, "Thank you, robins. I'll bear that in mind."

Just then a magpie flies down. The smaller birds scatter for cover, but the magpie isn't interested in harrying them. She addresses Connie, "We have an offer from the horses."

Connie is puzzled, but Corvo catches on at once. "How did you know?" he asks. "Are you with us?"

"Of course, we're with you, cousin," the magpie replies. "As for knowing, surely you know that all the Corvidae make it a point to be well informed." She turns to Connie. "My name's Manju. Word has got about regarding your plans and many of us want to help. We know you want stable gossip, but if the horses co-operated and won or lost in accordance with your bets, you would do far better."

"Brilliant!" cries Connie as she takes in Manju's offer. "I was going to leave the casinos and the racing till later, but Royal Ascot's coming up soon. If you wouldn't mind coming around to my house this evening, I can give you a list of the races I'll be betting on. We could make millions. Ludo, I need to use your name. Kams, yours as well. I probably need everyone's names to maximise our winnings without causing suspicion." Connie beams at Manju.

"No problem. See you later," Manju replies and flies off. How does she know where Connie lives?

Corvo sees me wondering. "Nobody knows what the magpies know," he tells me. "They've been collecting information for its own sake for millions of years, well, since they evolved."

Jack looks up from his phone to tell us there's a message from India. Should it come to war, the cows are offering to copy the robins. They'll be the vanguard. Nobody will harm them – at least not while anyone is watching.

"How did they hear about our plans so quickly?" I ask.

"Oh Jack's been texting," Juniper says. "I've already given him some names and numbers."

We look at each other, finding it hard to believe that all this is happening. Ludo and Gulliver take Corvo's drawing and the draft Manifesto and the Master Plan. Jack wants digital copies right away to flood the internet. Connie and Sybil go into a huddle about the racing. I didn't know Sybil was a betting woman. And Corvo and Kams whisper together in their capacities as Head of Intelligence and Home Secretary, in voices so low that they find it hard to hear themselves. Eventually they all disperse and Sybil and I begin to clear up; but the small birds want bread crumbs, also cake crumbs. So Sybil and I set out the remains in bowls for them.

11

Why do they think intelligent life has to be alien?

That night I snuggle up to Sybil and she puts an arm around my shoulders and tries to soothe me, but I can't sleep. How did I get into a revolution? All I ever wanted was to be with Sybil, make language malleable and write a good poem. "Sybil," I say, even though she's half-asleep, "I can see fracture lines spreading across the globe. What's going to happen?"

"Don't worry about it," she murmurs sleepily, "Go to sleep. Once we've begun we can't put the genie back in the bottle."

"Or the steam in the kettle," I add dolefully.

"Or the pink in the petal," comes a voice from outside.

"Is that you, Manju?" I call out to her. In a way it's comforting to hear her voice.

"Yes, it's me," she replies. "Why aren't you asleep?"

"I was puzzling over something. If we're all on the same side and we're all nice creatures and like each other, shouldn't we be refraining from eating each other?"

"Who said anything about all of us being nice all the time?" She sounds genuinely puzzled. "I'll tell you a story," she goes on. "It's a moral story."

"You mean it has a moral?" I ask.

"Not exactly," Manju replies. "It tells you how to behave yourself." She begins:

BEING NICE

There was once a woman who was discontent; she felt she ought to be better. She started by trying to be kind to animals. 'Sea cucumbers,' she muttered. 'Not much to be said for them. And they don't have much to say for themselves. They roll about on the ocean floor, and neither time nor tide makes any difference. They are nondescript.' When she examined herself, she found she was unable to say anything good about them.

'Perhaps I should start closer to home and find a creature I can actually engage with.' She walked down to the bottom of the garden and rolled back a stone. She had once come across a toad lurking there. Sure enough he was still there. As she peered at him, the toad shrank back. Perhaps if he didn't move, she wouldn't see him? But she knew a toad when she saw one. Would it count as friendliness if she patted the toad? She stretched out a hand. The terrified toad made himself as small as possible; she, on the other hand, was overcome by the thought of his slimy skin. She snatched back her hand.

'If only the toad hadn't been quite so ugly,' she sighed. 'But then there would have been no point in being nice to a beautiful creature. That would have been easy, though I don't think I would want to pet a tiger or a lion, however splendid.' As she wandered back, she nearly stepped on a small snake. She started back. 'No, I don't think it would be sensible to be kind to a snake,' she told herself. 'But then to whom should I be kind?'

In the end she settled for being kind to whomever she came across, but only when she felt like it and if she could manage it. 'I'm like everyone else,' she admitted. And having got used to being ordinary, it occurred to her that sea cucumbers might not be altogether lumpish and toads might not be all that slimy.

"Do you mean I shouldn't try to be nice?" I ask diffidently.

"I mean, take a good, hard look at yourself first," Manju retorts. "And be quiet. Get some sleep!"

In the end I fall asleep. I dream I'm holding a multicoloured ball and it explodes in my hands. And in the dream I wake up Sybil to ask what it means. She's impatient with me. "Don't be such a cry baby," she says. "That's not the planet. That's only the world with all the arbitrary boundaries marked on it." I blow my nose and while still in the dream I make myself a cup of tea. Then I wake up and find I do want a cup of tea. Through the window I can hear the dawn chorus. It sounds more muted than usual. It's nearly time to get up anyway.

There's no milk for my tea and no milk bottle on the doorstep.

"The cows are practising," a blue tit tells me.

"Practising?"

"Civil disobedience," adds the tit helpfully, "reducing their milk, so that when the time comes they'll get it right."

I take that in. "Were you practising as well this morning?" I ask.

The blue tit nods. "A kind of Work to Rule," she says. "Cutting down on birdsong. Leaving out the grace notes. Oh, and Connie and Manju are coming over straight after breakfast, so that Sybil can help them set up the bets. And Jack would like you to go over and help him sort out the text messages and emails. He's got millions and zillions of offers of help. And can I have some peanuts please?"

I give the blue tit some peanuts and make breakfast. Sybil comes down. Just seeing her cheers me up. She kisses me good morning. "Have you stopped fretting?" she asks. I mumble something. I don't know. Perhaps I have. Perhaps all this can be accomplished without bloodshed? Just by withholding milk and birdsong? Connie and Manju arrive soon afterwards; they settle down with Sybil to work out a plan.

As I clear the breakfast things, I hear Connie saying, "The fastest way to make a lot of money is by placing an accumulator bet – betting on the winner in all six races and getting it right. The horses just have to decide who wins which particular race. The trouble is winning such a bet attracts a lot of attention, so we had better do some doubles and trebles as well, use different names and scatter our bets among various courses."

Manju is enjoying this. "It beats collecting coins," she says.

They study the racing forms. "On the whole, best let the favourites win, except once in a while," Sybil murmurs. "It will attract less attention." They work slowly and methodically with Sybil making a list of races and horses and winners on her laptop.

"What about betting on a horse coming in second or third?" Manju asks.

"Too fiddly," Connie replies. "Let's just make a quick clean sweep and make a few million. We'll register as a company, The Good-Hearted Gardeners PLC, with all of us as directors. Then with the information you give me, I'll invest in the stockmarkets and the money markets too. By the end of the week we should be billionaires and able to fund our operation easily."

Sybil looks at Connie in wonderment. "In a week?" she says. "What if the governments start printing money, which is what they usually do when they get into trouble, and make money cheap? Then what will we do?"

"Buy gold," replies Connie. "Buy property. Don't worry about it, Sybil. If we have to, we'll just buy the governments."

I take a little longer than I need to over washing dishes because I can't believe what I'm hearing. But it turns out that is exactly what Connie does – she makes billions, and it doesn't even take her a week. Meanwhile, I finish the dishes, tell Sybil I'm going to Jack's and head out. There's more dog poo on the streets than usual. Civil disobedience?

At Jack's, Kams lets me in. I remember she had promised to help Jack. She's sitting at a table with six smart phones arranged in front of her, Jack's nearby on a swivel chair surrounded by computers.

"We can't cope," she confesses helplessly.

I'm amazed. Kams admitting defeat? It makes me very confident.

"What seems to be the problem?" I ask. "Too many offers of help?"

They can't speak. They manage to nod.

"Categorise," I tell them. "By species," I add when they still look blank.

"But where to begin?" Jack wails. I've never heard him sound quite so feeble. I suppose if I had a zillion messages, I would also be overwhelmed.

"Start with the ones likely to be the most helpful. We already have the crows, the magpies and the gulls on side. Do a search, and tell all the birds to coordinate with Corvo, Manju or Gulliver."

It takes Jack a minute or two to do all that. He's starting to feel better.

"What if the smaller birds are afraid of Manju?" Kams protests.

"So much the better," I reply in my new role as Efficient and Ruthless Problem Solver. "It will be all right. She'll deal with them."

"Jack," I ask, "how do the birds access the internet?"

"Sympathetic humans," he replies briefly.

I nod and carry on. "Next the mice and rats. Search for the words 'Paris' and 'King'. I'll never forget seeing them in the Metro – a river of bodies. We'll need them as allies. Anything from them?"

Jack searches and finds a message. It says:

Word has reached us of your noble revolution, and I, Rhodomont, King of the hosts inhabiting the Paris underworld, offer my services and those of my people. Deploy us in whatever way is most useful. We can cut through cables, shimmy up skyscrapers (albeit one floor at a time) and function as spies and messengers. When we choose we are almost entirely invisible, though in this regard I must confess the mice surpass us. Vive la Révolution! Vive les Rats! Vive les Souris! Vive everybody except bullies and braggarts!

Whew! It dawns on me we might actually reach Stage Three – Open Warfare – and that I'm supposed to be Defence Secretary. "Ask him if he would please coordinate all the rodents and make it their task to infiltrate the arsenals and make as many weapons as possible unusable. Cut wires, dampen gunpowder, mess up gun sights, sabotage gun barrels, destroy drones and anything else they can think of," I say to Jack.

Jack looks at me in surprise. Then he too realises that it may come to war and gets to work. Kams as Home Secretary sends a message to Corvo through a junior crow asking for intelligence on the location of weapons.

Jack's got the hang of being a superfast administrator and is even looking the part. He glances up from one of the computers, "There are a few hiccups. Some of the telephone lines in Mumbai are down. The mice there thought they needed practice …"

"Par for the course," I say cheerfully.

Jack turns to Kams. "Collect all the text messages into one or more files and send them to me. I'll run similar searches on them and give them back. That should help."

"What about the emails and messages from people?" he asks me.

"Sort out the ones from the organisations Juniper mentioned," Kams suggests, "And send a message to all the rest saying they should get in touch with the local branch of these organisations."

Jack nods. "Then there are a number of emails here from a group calling themselves 'Homo Supremacists'. They seem to think unfriendly aliens have invaded the earth and taken over the bodies of some of the animals. Such animals can be spotted by their ability to speak English. They want members of their organisation to capture these creatures for interrogation, but if that's not possible, to shoot them on sight. Should we reply to them?"

I shake my head. "Why do they think aliens from outer space converse in English?"

"And why do they think intelligent life has to be alien?" Kams adds.

Jack shrugs, but we decide that we ought to send out a warning to the birds, the mice and the other creatures:

If any humans try to speak to you in Pidgin English, don't correct their English. Play dumb. They'll try to capture you if they think you're an alien.

"It sounds mad," Kams says doubtfully. "Well, as long as they don't trust these people."

I go home for lunch. Sybil and I spend the rest of the afternoon running around racecourses placing bets. We return with a carload of money which we deliver to Connie. Once home, we have soup and rolls, and fall into bed exhausted. At about midnight we're woken up by Corvo tapping at the window. We let him in.

"Urgent meeting, right away. At Kams. Under the ash tree to consult Emma," he tells us. "All sorts of rumours are going round the world. We haven't got two weeks. Anything could happen."

"Can't it wait till the morning?" Sybil murmurs.

"Emma's nocturnal," Corvo replies. And that settles that.

We throw on some clothes and jump into the car. On the way I wonder whether Stage One – Passive Resistance – has begun or whether we are in Stage Two already and should be taking Proactive Measures. I say so to Sybil.

"I don't know," she replies. "As Culture Secretary should I be preparing counter propaganda? Or is the truth enough?"

I don't know what to say. It hasn't been so far.

12

Even a skinny cow outweighs a policeperson

When we get to Kams, she tells us that Emma is doing her nightly rounds and won't be back for another hour. We go inside to wait for Emma. It's the same room in which the Good-Hearted Gardeners interviewed us. Kams opens the window. I look around. I suppose we are still the Good-Hearted Gardeners, though Ludo informs us that MI5 have given us a month's salary and fired us; they feel we are not effective enough.

It's just as well. There are various Conspiracy Theories doing the rounds. Ludo says that according to one theory, teaching animals English is an MI6 plot.

"They're supposed to be acting on direct orders from Downing Street," Kams adds.

"There's a view on some media sites that it's the aliens. They are teaching the animals English," Jack puts in.

"And others are muttering that the animals have been able to speak English for a very long time and don't need the aliens or MI6," Juniper says with a smile.

"But the Indians don't believe a word of it," I tell them. "They're saying that when animals have chosen to speak, it has always been in Sanskrit, sometimes in Pali. Why would they be walking about talking English? It doesn't make sense."

"And there's another story," Kams informs us, "that the aliens have given the British a serum which allows the animals to learn English. The Russians want it banned as a biological weapon or a chemical one, but the Chinese don't as they say they've developed a serum of their own. As proof they've produced a Mandarin-speaking panda."

"I've known many Mandarin-speaking pandas," Sav offers shyly. "They pick up the local language – as well as English, of course. They even compose in it."

"Oh, and I heard," Kams interjects, "that in Chennai, a group of elephants led by their matriarch marched into the city and dismantled the platform of a politician who was fulminating against English. Then they marched back into the forest again."

"Are elephants anglophile?" Sybil asks.

"I don't know," Kams replies. "They may have been annoyed because the politician and his followers were making such a noise, or perhaps it's just another canard."

We smile at the stories being spread about, but underneath it all we're anxious.

"Things are happening too fast," Juniper says soberly. "We can't wait till the end of the month. The question is, what should we do?"

Just then Emma flies in, followed by Manju, Gulliver and Corvo, who station themselves behind her. She takes the head of the table, blinks at us and speaks: "The latest information, please."

"There are reports from villages nearby that sheep are grazing in football fields. From Australia there's news that kangaroos are leaping over parked cars, while emus do the can-can, and at the Sydney Opera House currawongs have taken over the brass section, magpies the woodwinds, and sulphur crested cockatoos the entire chorus. And in North America the blue jays have set up such a racket, that no one can think," Gulliver tells her respectfully. "We've also heard that fish have been liberated and trawlers overturned in the North Sea. There's a shortage of dairy products everywhere. The bazaars and the supermarkets are nearly empty. Cables have been cut, wires disconnected and pipelines damaged. In many places there is no electricity, and the internet is down intermittently so we don't always know what is happening. The relay network we gulls set up has provided some information, and we have also had help from the pigeons. Some governments have tried to use carrier pigeons, but half the pigeons refused and the rest have delivered the wrong messages. Trains have stopped running, and cars have been abandoned for lack of fuel. Ships at sea are looking for harbour, and most aeroplanes are grounded. Oh, and there's bird poo everywhere and the hens aren't laying."

Emma takes that in. "Warn everyone that war is imminent. And make it clear we have to engage in guerrilla warfare. Despite our attempts at sabotage they will have weapons left. We have none."

She turns to Corvo, "Have you located their arsenals?"

"Most of them, Madame Emma. Serenissima, our Queen, had already thought of it and the work was under way. We have forwarded the information to Rhodomont, who in turn has sent it on to various well-placed colleagues," Corvo answers.

"Excellent," Emma continues. "Let us hope they don't use nuclear weapons. Connie, disburse the money you've collected and let everyone buy what they need before the banks crash and money becomes irrelevant – at least for a time. You will all have to go underground soon. Acquire a safe house in which everyone can hide. Gulliver, setting up the relays was extremely efficient. Well done. Keep them functioning."

Gulliver is so chuffed by praise from Emma that he nearly falls over. "Thank you, Madame Emma. We birds probably won't need to hide. To human beings one gull looks very like another. It will be all right."

"Or not," Emma tells him. "They've been known to commit indiscriminate slaughter. Be careful. Whenever possible, stay out of sight."

"Should we deliver the Manifesto to the national governments and ask them to agree terms with our representatives?" Juniper asks. "Isn't there a chance that agreement might be reached and war avoided? After all, saving the planet is in the interests of everyone."

Emma looks at her for two long seconds. "Juniper," she says quietly, "and the rest of you, try to accept that the war has already begun, and human beings are not a rational species. Make your request for an Entente Cordiale to the governments at noon tomorrow, but do not be surprised if it is met with fury. How will you deliver it?"

"I will deliver it!" Manju declares. "I will nail it to the door of 10 Downing Street! And if I knock myself out, well, I'll pick myself up again. It's in a good cause, a great cause. And my fellow magpies will do the same in every country."

Some of us can't help cheering. Emma frowns. I wonder if she's going to scold us for levity, but she looks sad. "You haven't taken it in, have you?" she says gently. "Goodbye. Look after yourselves. Keep me informed." She leaves.

"We've already got a safe house deep in the country," Connie tells us. "Manju found it. You'll have to leave quietly. They've probably got your licence plates. I'll send directions for getting there tomorrow."

Corvo, Gulliver and Manju leave "Have to warn everyone," Corvo explains.

The rest of us just sit there for a moment looking at each other. We're supposed to be in charge, but we don't even know what to think.

"Why does Emma think we haven't even taken it in?" Juniper mutters.

"Because you haven't," Corvo tells her, flying back in through the window. "I will tell you a story about a human child and a crow. Perhaps then you'll understand."

WISH ME SOMETHING GOOD

The small child picking through the rubbish heap had made friends with a crow. They used to meet there almost every day.

'You realise that we are nothing but scavengers,' the crow remarked by way of conversation.

The child glared. 'Yes, but if you were a magic crow, you could grant my wish and we could be something different.'

'All right,' agreed the crow. 'I'm a magic crow. What do you want?'

'I want to be a Queen. A grand one. An Empress, sole ruler of all I survey.'

'You mean the rubbish heap?' asked the crow.

'No! Let the rubbish heap disappear!'

The crow obeyed and now they were just standing on a piece of ground.

'What about me?' asked the crow.

'You can wish yourself into anything you like,' replied the child. 'Why don't you?'

'I can't,' said the crow. 'I do the magic and you do the wishing. Wish me something good.'

The little one was a good-hearted child. 'All right,' she told the crow. 'You can be an emperor.'

And so the two of them whizzed about the world and played happily together. Other people, other birds and many other creatures looked at them in wonder. 'Why are you so happy?' they asked. 'Why are you so rich? What's your secret? Will you share it with us?'

'Of course, we'll share it,' the child replied. 'You can be empresses and emperors too.'

But when she asked the crow to turn everyone into an empress or an emperor, the crow shook his head. 'I'm sorry, Little One, I can't help. I'm only one crow.'

'Let's ask all the crows to help,' replied the child.

'Not all the crows, and not all the mynas and not all the sparrows, indeed, not all the birds in the wide world can accomplish this,' he said sorrowfully.

'Well, who can?' demanded the child.

'Everyone,' answered the crow. 'Everyone working together.'

'That's easy then!' cried the child. 'That's what everyone wants, isn't it?' to which the crow said nothing at all.

"You mean …?" Juniper asks.

"Yes!" Corvo tells her and flies out again.

Once home, Sybil makes a pot of tea – no milk. We sip it slowly.

"Sybil," I say at last, "I'm not sure I want to save the planet."

"Nor am I," she replies with a wan smile.

"But if we don't save the planet, we will die, so will everyone else – eventually."

"Yes."

"So we should try to save it?"

"Yes."

"What about species loyalty?"

"Do you feel it?"

"Not much, but there is our conditioning. I would rather eat bacon than sliced human being."

"If the war happens, or even if there's a peace treaty, I don't think we can go on eating meat."

"All right, no meat. I don't want to eat Corvo or Gulliver or Manju. And I wouldn't even think of eating Emma. She would probably —"

"Eat you first," Sybil finishes for me. "Still, I understand what you're saying. There are aspects of human supremacy and species privilege I quite enjoy – clean sheets, soft pillows."

"Heating in the winter."

"A good supply of groceries."

"Fuel for the car."

"The internet."

"The telephone."

"Washing machines."

"Would we have to give up all of it?"

"Some of it."

"And sleep in the woods? I don't even like camping!" I know I sound petulant. I don't know how to sound.

"And do we have to reap the harvest and till the soil?" I demand. "I don't know how to do it."

"Perhaps not," Sybil replies. "There are things about farming that are not eco-friendly. Still, one can hope … I began a poem," she continues.

"I replied to it."

"And I replied to your reply."

We look at the poem.

IN A WORKING PARADISE
There may be a place
      where bees go about
tending cells, collecting pollen,
        stashing honey;
while in the wide world
      nothing bad happens.
It's just another
      summer's day.

Don't bees die?
      Do the seasons not change?
Does the lion snuggle up
      to the woolly lamb?
And then does the lion
      eat the lamb?
Or does the stupid lion starve to death?

Bees die, some carry on
      to a reasonable age.
In a working paradise, even lions
      are allowed to live,
but there is no war
      and no one is exploited.

Perhaps she's right. Even if we can't have perfection, a working paradise would be a huge improvement.

"Will there be time for poetry?" I ask.

"Why not?" Sybil says. "Anyway, no earth, no poetry."

"If we survive, who will be writing for whom?" I demand.

"I don't know," Sybil replies. "I suppose you will be writing for Corvo and Manju, probably for Gulliver. And they'll be writing for us. Here's one of Manju's poems."

MAGPIE APOLOGIA

They are suspicious of us.

                       I can understand that.

We eat other birds.

                    And we're larger than most —

it creates mistrust.   Are we predatory?

                         Yes, of course.

But given that failing,

                 we are handsome birds.

So she's worried too. I open my mouth to say something, but Sybil interrupts, "Come on. Let's go to bed. It's late. It will be a long day tomorrow."

We fall asleep for what seems like only a moment. Corvo is at the window, knocking impatiently. We let him in. If we are to live in harmony with other species, I think sleepily, houses will have to be designed differently. Doors and windows will be interchangeable.

"What is it?" I ask rubbing my eyes.

"Something significant has happened. We think it's a sure sign of what's to come."

We wait for more.

"Cows have been attacked in India," Corvo tells us.

"What?"

"Cows have been attacked in India," he repeats slowly. "In broad daylight."

"Impossible," I say.

"What happened?" asks Sybil.

"You know that in India cows walk wherever they like, and sit down whenever they like; sometimes half a dozen or so can be found in the middle of a highway. The traffic swirls around them. Well, in order to practise Passive Resistance, they decided to do this in large numbers on the streets of Mumbai.

The government sent the police, and the police did their best to push them and pull them and move them along. They got nowhere. Even a skinny cow outweighs a policeperson. So then the government decreed that the cows were no longer cows, they had been taken over by aliens; and the fact that they could speak English was a clear sign. It was therefore all right to open fire on them. Some of the police did, and some refused; but the sight of cows being shot at was too much for the people of Mumbai. They erupted in indignation and attacked the police. There's a riot going on, and Mumbai would be in flames were it not for the fact that it's the rainy season and it's pouring buckets."

He pauses for breath. "You're right," I say. "If Indians can fire on cows, anything is possible."

"Which is why you must pack your things. Connie is sending a van tomorrow at one o' clock to take you to the safe house. Once our proposal is delivered, we're no longer safe. I have to get on with telling the others. It's likely that the party calling themselves Homo Supremacists, Soupies for short, will take the offensive. You are prime targets."

"We? Prime targets?" I repeat faintly.

"Don't you understand?" He's trying to be patient. "As they see it, you constitute a threat – you're trying to overturn the world order."

Corvo takes off. We forget about sleep, and think about what to take with us.

13

Soupies and Muties

We fill cardboard boxes and suitcases. We wonder whether we should pack food. Will there be provisions at the safe house? How long will we be there? By twelve thirty we're almost done. Manju will have nailed our Manifesto to the door of No. 10. How will the politicians react? We grab a bit of lunch. Cardboard boxes and suitcases are piled all around us. We've switched off everything, and are making sure the windows are closed, when the little robin hops in.

"Leave now," she tells us. "Juniper and Sav have parked the van at the back. They're coming for you in sleek, black cars. The men are carrying rifles."

"Who is coming for us?" Sybil asks.

"Don't know," says the robin. "Corvo said something about The Supremacists. But don't worry about it. We'll cover your back."

Just then Corvo, Juniper and Sav burst in. Juniper and Sav start hauling our luggage.

"Leave now," Corvo tells us. "Don't worry. We've got pots of paint to deal with the enemy."

Pots of paint? Just as we are being hustled through the back door, we hear the sound of gunshots, volley after volley. I turn back and see robins lying on the ground, some shot through, some torn apart – hundreds of them lying on the grass. They thought they wouldn't be shot at. I want to go out and shout 'No!' at the gunmen, but I'm a coward. I let Sav push me back. We jump into the van. Sybil is slumped in a corner, unable to talk, her face white. As we drive away, we hear sirens. Police?

Later, banners are made of robin redbreast covered in blood. Later, when accounts are written, they will call this The First Atrocity. There were many more atrocities on both sides. This was the one that made it clear to me which side I was on. I owe them.

Huddled in the van, we don't know what's happening until Corvo tells us much later. Sav is in the front with Juniper. She's driving furiously. We pick up Kams and a sleepy Emma and make for the safe house. It used to be a boarding school and before that a manor house. Connie has done well for us. She, Jack and Ludo are already there. Sav tells them about the massacre. Kams takes it particularly hard. "That Sybil's garden should become a place of slaughter," she mutters to herself.

Corvo, Manju and Gulliver arrive.

"The men in sleek cars were Supremacists – 'Human Beings Rule! OK?' – that sort of thing," Corvo tells us. "After shooting the robins, they were about to enter the house; but the police arrived, so they tried to get away. They couldn't. My friends and I tipped cans of paint over their windshields. Then the reporters arrived. Pictures and reports have been published everywhere. The Massacre of the Robins may be a turning point."

"Yes, but they're onto us," Ludo tells Emma. "They're calling us the Arch Conspirators of the Mutie Plot. MI5 are particularly annoyed."

"On the other hand," Jack says, "we've gained a lot of support. Demonstrations are going on all over the world with people telling their governments that they have to come to terms with The Party of Mutual Respect – that's us. It's the Soupies versus the Muties. Most of the governments don't know which side they are on."

We have wandered onto a battlefield. Juniper and Emma do their best to organise us. No time to mourn. We're given a cup of tea, put in front of a computer and told to coordinate activities pertaining to our departments all over the world. As Defence Secretary I have to make sure that Rhodomont is deploying his troops successfully and that the big cats and the pachyderms are kept out of confrontations. In spite of our efforts some hippopotamuses take it into their heads to block a river. This causes problems, but eventually the matter is settled without gunfire. Sybil, as Cultural Secretary, has to send out leaflet after leaflet trying to make it clear that we do not want to take over the world; we only want to save the planet. The rejoinder is always the same, "In order to do that, you are taking over the world, or at least trying to change the way human beings think and we don't see why we should change."

Jupiter and Sav have to talk to various species – sloths, anteaters and some spiders to mention a few – who say they want nothing to do with humans. It turns out Sav knows even more languages than Juniper. Comes of being a good listener, I suppose. Trees present a special problem. They take their time, and sometimes Sav has to sit under a tree for a whole day to get an answer. Mostly they say they will stay put – it is their nature, but they wish us well.

Jack and Kams have to make sure that at least some lines of communication are kept open. Ludo has to keep an eye on all the countries in the world and send help to the places where the revolution is having trouble. And Connie, as Chancellor, has to keep us going while economies founder everywhere. She and Manju do pretty well. And Corvo and Gulliver keep us informed. In the evenings we report to Emma.

Most of the time I feel out of my depth, and underneath it all I still see the robins lying on the grass.

Are we really going to change anything or have we merely disrupted everything? It's not just the news coming in that makes it clear the old systems are falling apart. The signs are there in small things. No meat, of course, and no milk in tea or coffee. Then no tea and no coffee. Not much in the way of food either. Brown rice and dandelion soup can get tedious. The manor house Kams has acquired has large grounds, and so we try to grow vegetables. We can't use pesticides, and certain fertilisers are out of bounds. Besides, just as the vegetables begin to sprout, we have to move again. The Soupies have located the Mutie headquarters. Soupies and Muties – it's ridiculous. But calling them Soupies doesn't make them less deadly. According to their propaganda we are The Party of Mutants – not properly human.

The next safe house is by the sea, which makes Gulliver happy. It's pleasant there. We don't spend all our time working on the revolution. There are breaks. One evening as Corvo, Gulliver, Sybil and I are sitting on the hillside looking at the waves, Corvo says to us, "You haven't given us a poem or told us a story for a long time. How about now?"

"Yes, how about it?" adds Gulliver.

Both want a story, and so it has to be about crows and about gulls. "You go first," Sybil says.

I take out my hip flask. I've been hoarding the whisky, but I share it sometimes, especially with Corvo who likes a drop or two. I pass the flask around, look across the bay and start.

A wily old crow, who liked to know what was going on and if at all possible to profit by it, had noticed that whenever a set of seven seagulls got together on the moored boats, they always had a good time. The sun shone, the sea was blue and the waves rollicked. Either the gulls were exceptionally lucky or they had to be extraordinarily clever. Clearly they knew something that the crow very much wanted to know.

Sybil takes over.

The crow kept a lookout and one day when the sun was shining and the boats were bobbing, the gulls appeared. As usual, they were laughing and chatting and seemed to be having an extraordinarily good time. The crow approached them in a diffident manner. She perched herself on the very end of a boat.

'Excuse me,' she said. 'Whenever I see you chatting on the boat, it's always good weather. What I want to know is how do you manage to control the weather?'

'Oh, we don't,' replied the gulls.

'Well, then how do you know when the sun will shine?' the crow demanded.

'We wait for it to shine and then we meet,' the gulls told her. They were looking anxious.

I carry on.

'Right,' said the crow. 'So the question is: which comes first, the gulls or the sun?'

'Right,' agreed the gulls, wanting to please.

'Now, tell me truth,' the crow went on. 'You seem to be an exceptionally lucky set of gulls. Is that why you're happy?'

By now the gulls were thoroughly muddled. They didn't know what to say.

'Here's what I'm asking,' the crow continued patiently. 'Are you happy because you're lucky?'

'Oh, Ma'am,' replied the gulls. 'We're lucky because we're happy.'

The crow frowned. Then she said, 'Thanks. I've got my answer,' and flew away.

It's Sybil's turn.

Soon afterwards the crow began to acquire a reputation for wisdom. People would ask, 'Please, Ma'am, will it be fine today?' The crow would gaze thoughtfully across the water. If the gulls were perched on the boats, she would nod solemnly, and if they weren't, she would shake her head. Soon people began to ask how they would fare: 'Please Ma'am, is today going to be lucky for us?' And for a small fee, the crow would answer: 'If you spot the Seven Seagulls, luck will follow.'

The people would go away and look for the gulls. If they spotted them, they'd feel happy, and if they didn't, they'd live in expectation. The crow would shrug, 'They're happy because they're lucky, or perhaps it's the other way around. Either way, I've got my fee and they have their answer.'

She did wonder sometimes about one thing though: was it luck or logic that had made her prosper?

"You've made the crow cleverer than us gulls," Gulliver protests.

"But we've made you lucky. Which is better?" Sybil says.

"The answer is obvious. We'll need all the luck and all the brains we're able to muster," a voice says suddenly. It's Madame Emma settling beside us. We didn't hear her come. "Is that whisky I smell?" she wants to know.

We offer her some. And Manju, who has just joined us, has some too. "What about me?" she demands. "Corvo and Gulliver have had several stories and a poem or two, but I've had nothing. Don't magpies deserve to be celebrated as well? Mostly we're maligned or regarded with suspicion."

"I could recite the 'Magpie Apologia'," I offer, but Manju demurs.

"You know it's said that originally all crows were white, but turned black when mourning for the crucifixion, all except magpies," Sibyl begins diffidently.

"Yes," Manju interrupts. "They say we were too hard-hearted to grieve."

"No, too hard-headed," Sibyl tells her. "Too wise. You knew about the resurrection."

"And," adds Emma gently, "when the time comes, the blue along your sides and the green in your tail will shine in splendour."

Manju looks pleased, but we all stare at Emma – so, she can be kind. We sit there for a while watching the sun dip down.

14

Living out our lives on the saved-in-time planet

It starts getting colder. Oil supplies have dried up. We light the occasional fire and tell ourselves we only do it infrequently. The revolution trundles on. After the killing of the robins, it's not as though the world said, "Oh, you're absolutely right. The Massacre of the Robins is too shocking to contemplate. We will do what is needed to stop global warming, and we will deal with our fellow animals with due respect." Despite the efforts of Rhodomont and his cohorts, the Soupies still have weapons. For us Muties the main tactic is sabotage. Accounts of carnage reach us, species against species, humans against humans. Communications break down. All over the world governments totter, tremble, can't make up their minds. In the end we have our revolution. It isn't quick, it isn't orderly. Sometimes it's not clear who is protesting about what and on which side. Finally we have a truce, a halt to hostilities and an agreement over division of territory.

At the negotiations Emma and Juniper insist that there be three zones. The First Zone, which Juniper tells them they are welcome to call The First World if they like, is to be set aside for humans only. No other living things are to be allowed there, except possibly trees, as they would find it difficult to uproot themselves. This gratifies the Soupies. They will enforce strict apartheid. No one can enter and no one can leave. And there is to be no interference at all in their affairs.

We consult the trees and they say they will stay where they are. "We will miss the bird life and the insects and the small mammals. Who will spread our seeds or pollinate us? But we take the long view," they tell us. "There will be insects, and the birds will return and so will everyone else – in time."

What happens, of course, is that the Soupies can't cope, not on their own. They haven't got an ecosystem and nothing flourishes and nothing grows. The diehards insist that it will all be fine, but refugees start trickling into the second zone. The theory is that in Zone Two everyone lives in harmony and there's mutual respect. The Good-Hearted Gardeners opt for this zone, of course, but we don't like the Soupies trickling in. They have the wrong attitudes and we feel they would spoil things for us. But they're refugees, and so some are allowed in, and some are turned away. We don't want to be nasty, but we're not very nice.

Sybil and I say to each other that although we have not established the earthly paradise, we have saved the planet.

Emma overhears us. "No, we've bought time," she tells us.

"And murder and mayhem sometimes happen. Feathers on the grass attest to this. None of us is perfect. The lion does not lie down with the lamb," Sybil adds judiciously.

But Emma isn't going to let us get away with anything. She wants to dot the i's and underline her sentences. "It's not that there are no killers among us. Some species kill, but unlike your lot, we tend not to do it needlessly."

Sybil and I hang our heads.

Emma's Third Zone excludes humans with the exception of

those who are indigenous to those regions. The polar caps, the Amazon forest and the bottom of the ocean are all included.

Sybil's old house has become a Place of Remembrance. We buy a new one near Kams. It's true it said in the Manifesto that private property was to be abolished. Well, that was changed slightly. The rules of private property apply only to the species that made them, not to anyone else. As for the rest of us, Jack moves in with Kams. Emma returns to her ash tree. She has unbent considerably and sometimes she's quite nice to us. And Sav and Juniper move in together. They set up a language school – for humans. And gradually, very gradually, Connie and Ludo become an item. Gulliver and Manju live on their own estate. Corvo tends to live near us. He likes bridge, and so does Manju. Sometimes we play together. The Good-Hearted Gardeners still meet.

The robins were killed in the old garden that was paradise for us for a short time. We have a different garden now. We look after it as best we can.

One day I say to Sybil, "If I'm just a grasshopper chirping in the grass and human consciousness is not at the centre of the universe, will you still like my poems?"

She nods. "Yes. We never were at the centre of anything. Will you still like mine?"

"Why not? We can be grasshoppers, budgerigars or bottle-nosed dolphins, and sing duets."

"And choral works," she adds.

"Living out our lives on the saved-in-time planet."

"Not claiming too much space."

"We can no longer dictate what happens."

"We never could. We'll have to be less egoistic."

"The blood of hundreds of robins breaks my heart. I cared about them."

"And therefore you write better poems."

"Will my poems matter as little as birdsong?" I ask.

"And as much."

"Will we have to please Serenissima and Emma and every-one else?"

"We'll have to try."

Sybil and I are probably as selfish and self-centred as most other creatures, but not more so. We grow older. And the love affair changes into a way of life, even a habit. We are each other's place of shelter.

Once it's realised that birds and beasts have speech, the whole notion of who is writing for whom shifts. Have we liquefied English? No, it has expanded beyond bursting point, beyond control. What about poetry then? For sloths we'll have to write in slow time, and for dragonflies encapsulate a whole lifetime. Our shift from the centre is more fundamental than Galileo's remapping. Everything we make must be left unsigned. Though my heart trembles, I begin again.

Acknowledgements

Boa Senior and *Bee on Ice* first appeared in *South Asia Focus,* Vol. 32, No. 2 (Spring–Summer) 2016, Weber State University, USA. *Vihaan and the Crow* was published in *CONVERSE: Contemporary English Poetry by Indians*, edited by Sudeep Sen (Cambridge, UK: Pippa Rann Books & Media, 2022). *The Sybil* appeared in *The Four Quarters Magazine* (Online) ISSN: 2349-6061 Vol. 4, No. 1 (April–May) 2015.

Books by Suniti Namjoshi available from Spinifex Press

Feminist Fables

The classic title by Suniti Namjoshi who is both elegant and subversive in creating new patterns of meaning through stories that are simultaneously spare and full of richness. An ingenious reworking of fairy tales from East and West.

ISBN 9781875559190

St Suniti and the Dragon

Where are good and evil to be found? What is the path to sainthood? Is it through poetry or good deeds? St Suniti talks to angels and flowers, dragons, saints and ordinary people in her quest. Suniti Namjoshi has original imagination full of surprises encompassing saints and wolves, Beowulf and Bangladesh, Grendel and Star Trek.

ISBN 9781875559183

Building Babel

Every retelling of a myth is a reworking of it. Every hearing or reading of a myth is a recreation of it. It is only when we engage with a myth that it resonates, becomes charged and recharged with meaning. And so it is in *Building Babel*, a book that re-engages with myth through the cyberworld, where worlds intersect and are transformed.

ISBN 9781875559565

Goja

Suniti Namjoshi traverses the cultures of the East and of the West. She muses on the patterns of her life, and of the impact of colonisation, both the resistances and the acceptances of it. Growing up in the ruling house of Maharashtra, the two most important relationships in her life were with her grandmother, the Ranisaheb, and with Goja, the servant woman who slept beside her bed. Then she moved to the West. In the US and Canada, she became just another brown-skinned immigrant without the privileges of her childhood.

ISBN 9781875559978

The Fabulous Feminist

It was on a sabbatical in England in the late 1970s that Suniti Namjoshi discovered feminism – or rather, she discovered that other feminists existed, and many among them shared her thoughts and doubts, her questions and visions. This collection brings together in one volume a huge range of Namjoshi's writings, starting with her classic collection, *Feminist Fables*, and her later work.

ISBN 9781742198217

Blue and Other Stories

Illustrated by Nilima Sheikh

Suniti Namjoshi, internationally acclaimed fabulist and poet, brings both depth and lightness of touch to *Blue and Other Stories*. Playful and gentle, each of these stories effectively traverses layers of myth to speak to both children and adults.

ISBN 9781742198392

Suki

In *Suki*, Suniti Namjoshi weaves a witty and delightful tapestry from threads of longing, loss, memory, metaphor, and contemplation. *Suki* is a lightly fictionalised memoir of one woman and her cat.

ISBN 9781742198880

Aesop the Fox

Aesop's fables are brought to life by the timely intervention of Sprite from the future, who prods Aesop into debate about the meaning of stories: are they for fun, or do they have the chance to change the world? This book offers a virtuoso display into how the building blocks of fables can enchant, enrage, enlighten and educate us all.

ISBN 9781925581515

If you would like to know more about
Spinifex Press, write to us for a free catalogue, visit our
website or email us for further information
on how to subscribe to our monthly newsletter.

Spinifex Press
PO Box 105
Mission Beach QLD 4852
Australia

www.spinifexpress.com.au
women@spinifexpress.com.au